BLACK FEATHER

NINJANS 2

Dave Kwan

DISCLAIMER

This book is a work of Fiction.
Names, characters, businesses,
places, events, locales, and
incidents are either the products
of the author's imagination
or used in a fictitious manner.
Any resemblance to actual persons,
living or dead, or actual events
is purely coincidental.

Book Cover Credit: Artwork by Nadtytok28 - Adobe Stock

File#: 385786512 JPEG 6000 x 4000px

This book is dedicated
to honour my deceased parents,
Raymond and May Kwan;
who adopted me and gave their love and care.
Their example of hard working immigrants
with personal sacrifice and open generosity,
provide me with a valuable legacy
to deeply cherish and fondly remember.

Thank you Dad and Mom!

CHAPTER ONE

The Ninjans Return

Otter and the fellow Ninjans stride past the perimeter trees and move deeper into the forest. After a number of paces, they stop to look back at the open clearing. Cutter, a mean wicked outlaw, sits propped up against a tree trunk - he's bleeding out, exposed and vulnerable. Blood seeps from the deep gash in his side and pools beside him. Vicious wolves surround him and creep closer and closer; growling, snarling - snapping their jaws. Saliva drips from their sharp teeth. The hair on their bodies bristled, the animals crouch low to the ground as they close in on their prey. Cutter is gripped with horror - the wolf pack can smell his fear - and the scent of fresh blood. The large black Alpha wolf edges forward and locks eyes with Cutter as he trembles and squirms. The Alpha wolf lets out a loud growl - then leaps. The wolf pack descend upon Cutter in a frenzy. He screams wildly as the wolves bite and tear into his flesh. The evil outlaw is no longer visible - covered up by the wolf pack. The Ninjans turn away and resume their direction. The warriors are muscular and agile and move swiftly over the forest terrain. Their pace is strong and steady with few breaks - all day and through the moonlit night and into the next day. It is late afternoon when Otter and the Ninjans arrive back in the Shoshone camp. The villagers throng the returning warriors as they walk to the Chief's large central tepee. The atmosphere is filled with excitement and jubilation! Chief Buffalo Sky and the Elders are standing outside. As Otter and the fellow Ninjans approach, the braves bow low to show respect to the Tribal leaders. By now, the entire Shoshone village are gathered, everyone energized and alert to the moment. Buffalo Sky sets his eyes on Otter and the Ninjans, and speaks, "How was the raid?" Otter replies. "The outlaws walk the earth no more!" All the Shoshone know full well the injustice and suffering caused by Cutter and his gang of outlaws when they killed and scalped the Shoshone hunters and fur trappers. Chief Buffalo Sky lifts his arm high in the air and the entire camp becomes still and quiet, all eyes on their Chief, everyone's ear ready to hear his words. Buffalo Sky looks out at his people and speaks with a loud clear voice, "Our fallen braves are avenged!" The Shoshone villagers erupt with cheers, cries of celebration, and loud yells of victory! The people crowd in to congratulate their Ninjan warriors. When the outpouring of gratitude subsides and the people disperse, Otter and his fellow Ninjans leave, each one going to his tepee.

On route to his place, Otter meets Yuji, Bright Star and little Kamatsu. Otter bows low as he greets his former Sensi and Ninja Master. Yuji bows in return and comments, "The Ninjans have a fine leader!" Otter smiles and replies. "That is because I had a great teacher." Bright Star grins at the friendly exchange. She reaches out and touches Yuji's arm, glances at Otter, then turns to Yuji and nods. Yuji is reminded of the couple's earlier talk, and asks the young man, "We want you to sit at our evening meal." Bright Star holding little Kamatsu on her hip, looks Otter in the eye and adds, "You would honour our tepee!" The young man is delighted at the invitation and grins, "Yes! Everyone knows your venison and bannock are the best in the village!" Bright Star's modesty makes her blush at the compliment. Yuji cheerfully remarks, "We can eat and talk as we did so many fires ago." Otter nods with a big smile, bows respect, and turns in the direction of his dwelling. Yuji and Bright Star stand and watch Otter leave, they are happy at Otter's acceptance. Around them, the camp is busy with mealtime, there's family activity at each tepee. As the afternoon sun begins to set - Yuji, Bright Star and tiny Kamatsu make their way home.

The small family walk past many dwellings to their tepee. Yuji lifts up the entry flap as Bright Star lowers slightly to carry Kamatsu inside. After his wife and son have gone within, Yuji steps inside and reaches behind to pull down the buckskin flap. Most Indian tepees, even those of other tribes, share a common design and construction. Fourteen to seventeen wooden poles from sixteen to eighteen feet long, are tightly lashed together at the top, then covered with a thick canvass that is secured to the wood frame. The top opening allows smoke to rise and escape, while inside, the people enjoy the fire for warmth, light and to cook meals. The open living space is designated - an area to prepare and cook food, a sleeping section, and a free space for family and visitors to sit, relax and talk. Any important objects or personal possessions are tied to the tepee interior that circles the family quarters. The beauty of a tepee is that it only needs wood poles and fabric, and the structure can be easily set up or taken down to relocate elsewhere. It was a simple and practical solution for nomadic Indian tribes that migrate in search of hunting and fishing grounds. Yuji and Bright Star's tepee was of this nature, it was where they showered tiny Kamatsu with love and care, and where they lived as a happy family in the Shoshone village.

Yuji takes Kamatsu from Bright Star so she can arrange the evening meal before Otter's arrival. The young wife and mother lays out the already cooked food in wooden and shallow gourd bowls. She sets out the fried bannock, an Indian staple that everyone enjoys from youngsters to older folks. Next, she places fresh hand-picked blueberries and raspberries in a gourd bowl. Bright Star picks up the cooked venison and lays the meat strips on a smooth cedar board, then she places the clay cups and clay pot of fresh water nearby. Yuji and Kamatsu keenly watch as Bright Star checks that everything is ready for their guest. Bright Star glances at her meal setting, then she looks at Yuji and nods with a smile, "The meal is ready. I hope he likes the venison?" Yuji replies, "No one cooks venison like you. Otter will eat well tonight." Tiny Kamatsu fusses a bit and puts out his little hand toward his mom, Bright Star reaches over and takes her son in her arms and cradles him and gently kisses his forehead. The tiny tot breaks into a big smile and grabs a lock of Bright Star's hair. Yuji stares at his beautiful wife and adorable son, lost in a sublime special moment. At that instant, the entry flap lifts and Otter announces his presence, "Otter is here!" Yuji replies, "Join us brother. You must be hungry!" Yuji and Bright Star welcome Otter with smiles and gesture that him sit beside them. Otter crouches as he steps into the tepee interior and walks a few paces and sits down cross-legged. The young warrior grins as his eyes fasten on the food items arranged before him. Bright Star gives Otter a shallow clay bowl and comments, "Your presence with us warms our hearts." Otter replies, "I've not eaten in two days, since we left camp to avenge our fallen braves." Yuji remarks, "Your mission was a success! You and the Ninjans rid the earth of those evil men." Yuji picks up Kamatsu as Bright Star dishes out food for their guest and old friend. Bright Star smiles as she heaps Otter's bowl with generous portions of venison, bannock and berries. She pours him a cup of water and sets the water pot aside. Once Otter has his food, Yuji and Bright Star pick up their bowls and get their meal items. The young mom takes little Kamatsu from Yuji and lays him on the blanket beside her. Otter's hunger is apparent as he ravishes and chews the venison strips enjoying every bite. He soon devours all his venison, bannock and berries. Bright Star grins at Otter's hearty appetite and takes his empty bowl and loads it with more food, and passes it to him. Otter smiles as he receives his second helping, and proceeds to feast as only a hungry young man can. They eat and relax like the good friends they are. Yuji finishes eating and sips his water as he quietly waits for Otter to complete his meal. Bright Star plays with Kamatsu to keep the tot occupied. Otter finishes eating and sets aside his clay bowl and takes a drink of water. Little Kamatsu reaches out to Otter and the young brave picks up the youngster. Kamatsu is intrigued with Otter's long hair and decorative trinkets and plays with them but soon becomes tired. Bright Star remarks, "He's sleepy. I will take him now." Otter hands Kamatsu to his mom and she carries him to the sleeping area, tucks him in for the night, and then returns. Bright Star and Yuji make eye contact, then Yuji looks at Otter and speaks, "My brother, we want you to train Kamatsu. My years and strength are fading - no one knows how long the ground will know his shadow." Otter is honoured but somewhat surprised, "Sensi. You are still strong." Yuji gazes fondly at the young warrior, "You were my best student. I must know that you, and you alone, will train Kamatsu when he is of age." Otter is quiet for a few seconds, glances over at the sleeping boy, then looks at Yuji and Bright Star and replies, "Sensi. I pledge to train Kamatsu - like you once trained me!" Yuji smiles relief, "Your words give me peace." As Otter sits quiet and reflects on what's been said, Yuji gets up and retrieves an object from under a blanket and returns and sits opposite Otter. Yuji unfolds an embroidered buckskin to reveal a large stunning Black Feather and hands it to Otter. The young warrior is wide-eyed and speechless! Otter's hand slightly trembles as he clasps the Black Feather and humbly bows. Otter remarks, "Sensi. This is too great an honour for me!" Yuji reaches out his hand to encourage his former trainee to lift upright, "You have proved yourself worthy many times. - It is my honour to give you the Black Feather!" Otter bows low and raises up, "Sensi. Arigato gozaimasu!" Yuji gazes at the young Ninjan leader and bows and replies 'go ahead' in Japanese, "Hai dozo!" Bright Star beams with happiness at Otter's pledge to train her son, and feels proud to have witnessed Otter receiving the highly regarded Black

Feather. Throughout the remainder of the evening, the three friends enjoy each other's company and conversation as they bask in the warm glow of the tepee fire.

CHAPTER TWO
Otter Trains Kamatsu

The seasons change as the warmth of summer gives way to the cool breeze of Fall. The colourful meadow flowers have wilted and the forest leaves turn yellow, brown and gold, and later, flutter from trees to carpet the ground during the days of Autumn. Soon, the forest has only bare trees with dead brittle leaves on the ground. A cold wind begins to blow and brings with it big snow flakes of delicate ice crystals, that dance in the air before landing on the ground to form a blanket of snow. All of Nature undergoes a transition, even the coats of wild animals change; the fox's red jacket becomes white fur, and the rabbit's brown beige appearance becomes that of fluffy white, allowing the small creature to safely hide in Winter's landscape. The black bear no longer looks for honey or forages all day long in the berry patch, the weighty bruin slumbers in deep hibernation in a secluded wilderness cave. The fast flowing rivers and the placid lakes become covered with frozen sheets of ice. At times, the frozen lakes and rivers crack and creak, making Indian hunters and trappers careful as they walk across the frozen surface, wary that the ice may break and they fall through into the frigid cold water. However, such seldom happens, because the American Indians know the forest and rivers from an early age. Indian people live in harmony with nature, respecting the animals, plants and bounty of their Tribal lands.

It is during the Springtime when Otter begins to teach Kamatsu hand-to-hand combat. The youth is quick, strong and agile, and poses a worthy adversary. Yuji and Bright Star smile as Otter and Kamatsu grapple, wrestle and jostle about, each trying to overpower and off-balance the other. Otter is breathing heavy as he battles the wiry teen. Otter grabs Kamatsu's arm to flip him, but the teen twists and turns to block Otter's attempt, then pivots to put Otter in a hold. Otter glances at Yuji and Bright Star and grins, then the Ninjan Master clutches Kamatsu's arm and swiftly spins the youth - right into a submission hold. Kamatsu groans as he struggles and strains to break free but cannot. Realizing he's defeated, Kamatsu taps surrender and Otter releases his young trainee. Once free and mobile, Kamatsu stands straight, faces his Sensi and bows low. Otter bows in return. Having concluded the training exercise, Otter puts his hand on Kamatsu's shoulder as the two walk toward Yuji and Bright Star. Otter remarks to his pupil, "You almost had me in that hold!" Kamatsu replies, "Why didn't it work? I used the right technique!" Otter responds, "Your hold was correct, but your body position was wrong - letting me to get free." A pondering expression comes over Kamatsu's face, then he remarks, "Now I see it! I should have positioned my right leg better and leaned back." Otter smiles acknowledgement, "Your arm hold and body position would have locked me good. Next time, remember!" Kamatsu nods with a grin. The two approach Yuji and Bright Star on the high ground, and bow. Yuji and Bright Star bow in return. Yuji remarks, "I see improvement since the last time." Kamatsu eyes his Teacher and replies, "Apparently not enough improvement, or my hold would have worked." Bright Star smiles and adds in a motherly way, "Next time my son." Otter looks at his old friends and comments, "Kamatsu has greatly improved from when we started. He's becoming more capable each time we train. (Otter grins) The day will arrive when I can no longer beat him.(Otter glances at the lad) I look forward to that day!" Bright Star speaks motioning with her hand, "Food in the tepee will help replenish two hungry warriors." Otter and Kamatsu nod their heads and smile. Kamatsu playfully remarks, "My Sensi may out fight me - but he can't out eat me!" The adults laugh at Kamatsu's words as they leave the training area.

The day dawns and rays of bright sunlight pierce the morning mist on the ground. Otter and Kamatsu stand in front of the wide forest tree, the trunk covered with small open dimples. Otter has a handful of Shuriken and turns to his teenage apprentice, "Arm position and finger grip determine the direction when throwing at your target. Watch me." Kamatsu's eyes lock in on how and where his Sensi holds the pointed metal star, and notes the Master's arm position and throwing technique. Otter flings his arm and releases a Shuriken at the tree. Whoosh! The metal star spins in a blur as it sails toward the trunk - Thud! The Shuriken strikes the trunk and the sharp metal point embeds deep into the wood. Otter glances at Kamatsu and remarks,

"Now, you try - remember to aim and release the Shuriken at the right moment." Kamatsu nods, adjusts his leg position for better balance, looks at the tree trunk, and flings his arm and opens his fingers - the black metal star spins and twirls toward the tree only to curve and miss the trunk completely. Kamatsu is stunned since he thought the Shuriken was going to hit the target. The young trainee looks over to his Sensi, and asked puzzled, "Master, How come I missed?" Otter copies how Kamatsu positioned his fingers and the way he flung his arm, and demonstrates the throw. As Otter throws, Kamatsu observes the star going straight at the trunk, then moves in an arc to miss the tree. Otter positions his arm and fingers in the proper technique - shows Kamatsu, then throws - the Shuriken twirls in blinding speed to sink deep into the trunk's perforated surface - Thud! Kamatsu's eyes light up as he realizes why his throw missed the tree and his Sensi's throw hit the target. Otter encourages his student, "Try again like I showed you." Kamatsu copies his Teacher's finger placement and arm position, takes a breath, then swings his arm and watches the Shuriken spin straight toward the tree and strike the trunk - sinking deep into the wood. Kamatsu smiles accomplishment and looks at his Sensi. Otter nods his head with approval and smiles, "Your throw was correct. Remember, finger grip and arm position determine the various ways to throw a Shuriken." Kamatsu nods tight lipped, he understands. For the latter portion of the training exercise, Otter instructs Kamatsu in the various ways to throw a Shuriken - depending on the target and the distance. For the rest of the morning, Kamatsu throws, retrieves, throws again, retrieves the Shuriken, and repeats this throughout the rest of the training session. Otter gazes up at the bright sun overhead and comments, "Time to stop - rest - and eat some food." Kamatsu is so focused on developing his throwing technique that he forgets how hungry he is. The lad turns to his Sensi with a grin, "Did you say food?!" Otter teases Kamatsu, "Yes! Food. I know teenagers are always hungry. (Smiles) It was like that when I was a teenager." Kamatsu teases back, "Oh! You were a teenager?" The man laughs, walks away, then turns and motions for the teen to come on along.

As the weeks, months and years pass by; Kamatsu grows taller, bigger, and more muscular. He is quick, agile, and more experienced with the Ninjan fighting techniques. Yuji and Bright Star observe as Kamatsu shows his ability with the various weapons. The young man masterfully spins and aims the chain dart to strike a small target - he capably handles and throws the tomahawk - and shoots black arrows and never misses the target - he swings and twirls the Ninjan war club with great competence - and displays his prowess in hand-to-hand combat with blocks, punches, strikes, kicks, throws and choke holds. Kamatsu has progressed mightily and has excelled in all manner of weapon and combat. Now, only the last phase of Ninjan training remains - swordsmanship. Otter begins Kamatsu by using the wooden sword and teaches the basics. Kamatsu is a fast learner and quickly shows competency with using the wood sword for defence and offence. His parents watch as Otter and Kamatsu spar against each other with their wooden sword - there is a flurry of action as both swing and block, thrust and deflect, chop and slice at their opponent. The Sensi has a tough challenge from his vigorous athletic apprentice. But as adapt as Kamatsu is, the young man is out manoeuvred by his Sensi, and Otter attacks with a flurry of swings, chops and blows that has Kamatsu backing up in defence. Finally, Otter spins his wood sword with such force that Kamatsu's sword flies out of his hand - leaving the young man weaponless and defeated. As Otter stands with the wood sword pointed at his student - Kamatsu nods and bows low to honour his Teacher, "Sensi. You have taken away my sword - I surrender!" Otter steps close to his student and comments, "You have outgrown the practice sword - Now, you will train with the steel Katana sword." Kamatsu bows and replies, "Arigato Sensi! I'm ready for your instruction!" Otter smiles at his student's improved ability and humble attitude.

It was on a breezy Autumn day when Otter walks to their training area. Otter carries two swords and wears his black Ninja outfit, Kamatsu is dressed in a white Ninja outfit. Arriving at the location, Otter hands Kamatsu a glossy white Katana sword to use for his Ninja training. The Sensi looks at his pupil, "You must learn how the steel sword feels in your hand - its weight and balance. First, we will start with a practice Kata - follow how I hold and use my sword." Kamatsu takes a quick breath and nods. Otter steps a few yards away for a safe distance, and positions himself and grips his shiny black Katana. Kamatsu copies his Sensi's body, arm and sword position, and waits. Otter looks at his student, then steps forward and slices downward at a 45 degree angle. He looks over at Kamatsu and nods. The young man copies his Teacher's move and sword slice, then glances at Otter for his response. Otter nods his head and grins, then launches out with an upward left and upward right cut. Kamatsu follows suit. All during the morning, with the crisp Fall air making their breath show, Otter leads Kamatsu through the first training exercise with the steel sword. Over the next number of weeks and months, Kamatsu matches his Sensi perfectly. The two Ninja warriors move in synchronized manner like two field birds that fly through the sky, each keeping the same distance apart, each moving and turning at the same time. Anyone observing would see that both men hold their sword at the same angle, swing their blade at the same moment, and keep together as the two steel blades - swing, twirl and slice through the air at imaginary foes.

Now the moment has arrived when Otter feels Kamatsu is ready to spar with the Katana. Basking in the bright morning sunshine, Otter and Kamatsu face each other with steel sword in hand. Otter takes a battle stance and remarks to Kamatsu, "Whenever you are ready!" Kamatsu firmly grips his Katana and assumes a fighting position and locks eyes with his Sensi - then launches out with a barrage of swings, thrusts and chops. Otter's sword is kept busy blocking and deflecting Kamatsu's attack. The two quickly move around the flat training ground, shuffling their feet from one battle stance to another. Otter eyes his pupil, then attacks with a flurry of strikes that keeps Kamatsu's sword on the defence. The sparring session is intense, both warriors seeking to conquer their opponent. There's a sudden lull as Otter and Kamatsu stop to catch their breath. Otter comments to his student, "You handle the Katana very well!" Kamatsu smiles and replies to his Sensi, "That is because I had an excellent Teacher! The older man raises up the palm of his free hand, "Let's stop for today. (Otter grins) There will be many more days to spar." Kamatsu nods and they both leave the training ground and head toward the village tepees.

CHAPTER THREE
Kamatsu The Ninjan

In a lovely forest setting, Yuji and Bright Star stand side by side, they no longer have the shiny black hair of yesteryear, now their hair is fully grey - the colour of old people. Their skin no longer smooth and supple as in their youth, now their faces are wrinkled and etched from the experiences of life. On this special day, their eyes sparkle with hope, their spirits soar, their hearts are filled with joy, as they observe Otter and Kamatsu, both dressed in Ninjan black outfits. Otter is now middle-aged, and Kamatsu is a full grown man. The two warriors respectfully kneel across from each other on the large ceremonial straw mat with bouquets of flowers that decorate the edge of the woven surface. In the middle between them, a glossy black Katana sword sits nestled in its wooden cradle. A small ceramic bowl with burning incense sticks sits at one side of the Katana, and on the other side lays an embroidered buckskin pouch and a small bronze bowl and wood stick. Yuji and Bright Star watch with anticipation.

Otter looks at his graduate, bows and lifts up. Kamatsu bows and returns upright. Otter clasps the ceramic bowl and extends it toward Kamatsu, and circles the burning incense and sets the bowl aside. Otter looks at Kamatsu and chants, "Bushi - Chigiri!" Kamatsu bows low and holds steady and replies, "Chigiri Sensi!", then he lifts up. Otter looks at Kamatsu, reaches with both arms to pick up the Katana and extends it. Kamatsu reaches out to clasp the Katana and holds it. Otter release his grip and Kamatsu holds the Katana with both hands, brings the sword against his chest, then bows low and remains still. Otter keeps his eyes on the bowed graduate and speaks in an authoritative tone, "Bushi - Ninjan! Bushi - Ninjan!" Kamatsu clutching the sword and bowed, replies, "Aho! Chigiri Ninjan! Aho! Chigiri Ninjan!" Otter smiles at Kamatsu's firm response and picks up the wood stick and strikes the bronze bowl to emit a ringing sound that envelopes their forest setting. Kamatsu lifts upright with a sparkle in his eye as he holds the Katana. Otter, his lifelong Sensi, smiles and stands to his feet. Kamatsu rises and stands to his feet to face his Sensi. Otter remarks, "You are no longer a trainee - an apprentice. From this day onward - you are a Ninjan!" Otter bows respect to Kamatsu and Kamatsu bows in return. Kamatsu smiles victoriously and turns to look at his father and mother who have witnessed his Graduation Ceremony. Bright Star is happy and crying with tears flowing down her face, and Yuji stands tall and proud with a big smile.

CHAPTER FOUR
Chief Buffalo Sky Dies

It is an overcast sky the day the Shoshone villagers gather at the Tribe's burial grounds, their hearts are sad because their great Chief Buffalo Sky has died. The Chief's lifeless body rests high up on the wood burial tower. His rifle, tomahawk, hunting knife, bow and quiver of arrows, lay beside him. The entire Shoshone tribe stand in a circle to surround the burial tower. The Tribal death drums pound as the people watch Eagle Feather, now an old man, chant Shoshone prayers to the Great Spirit as he casts white powder into the air. Everyone observes in silence, no one talks, not even the little children; there's only the sound of the wind, Eagle Feather's chanting, and the beating of the drums.

Five fires have now passed since Buffalo Sky has died, and the Tribal Elders meet at the large central tepee to decide who should be the next Chief. Inside the tepee, the Council Fire burns bright and makes the faces of the Elders and lead warriors glow. There is much discussion among the Elders. Outside the tepee, all the Shoshone braves stand in clusters, talking among themselves about who will become their new Chief. The entry flap of the tepee lifts up and Eagle Feather steps out. All the braves stop their conversations and everyone looks at the old warrior. Eagle Feather scans across the throng of braves and speaks, "Tomorrow we gather to honour our new Chief!" The braves realize the Tribal Council have reached a decision and they begin to disperse toward their homes. Eagle Feather lifts up the entry flap and steps back inside.

It is a sunny morning and all the camp have assembled near the central tepee. The Elders stand in the middle of an open area and the Shoshone people surround them. Eagle Feather holds the tribe's War Lance, the weapon will belong to the new Chief. An Elder beside him holds the Chief's Feathered Bonnet, the tribe's visible symbol of honour and leadership. The mass of people are abuzz in lively chatter about who will be the new Chief. Eagle Feather lifts up the War lance and all the people stop talking and rivet their eyes on the respected warrior. He looks about and lifts his voice, "The Tribe's Elders have made their decision. Now, you, the Shoshone people, must show your acceptance. Only when the Elders and the people accept the decision, can he become the new Chief." Eagle Feather pauses and gazes around at the faces of the villagers. The grownups and young ones understand his words. Eagle Feather steps out from the Elders and stands alone, and calls out, "The Elders decide that Bear Claw will be our new Chief!" Bear Claw is standing with Gold Flower, Yuji and Bright Star. He looks at them and they smile proudly. The seasoned warrior steps out from the group of villagers and walks to stand next to Eagle Feather. As the Elders and the entire camp watch, his old friend Eagle Feather fits the Feathered Bonnet on Bear Claw's head and hands his the War Lance. As Bear Claw stands wearing the Chief's Feathered Bonnet and holding the War Lance, Eagle Feather steps aside and points to the Tribe's new Chief - and all the Shoshone people, from the old to the young, erupt with loud cheers, and cries of victory and celebration. The Elders have a contented smile that they picked well. With the entire camp visibly and vocally honouring their new Chief, Eagle Feather leans close to his lifelong friend and remarks, "I am happy for you old friend! You were the best choice as our new Chief. (Pause) The Great Spirit will help you lead our people!" Bear Claw looking majestic in the Chief's Feathered Bonnet and holding the tribe's War Lance, looks out at the happy Shoshone people, then smiles and nods to his friend, "I will need the Great Spirit very much!" An Elder holds up his arm and the boisterous people ebb to a silence. The Elder speaks out with joy, "Tonight, we will sing, dance, eat - and celebrate our new Chief Bear Claw!" The Shoshone villagers break out with cheers and cries of happiness. As the merry people disperse, The Elders, Eagle Feather and Chief Bear Claw enter the tribe's central tepee; now the new home for Bear Claw and Gold Flower.

Deep in the forest, amid the tall pines streaked with shafts of sunlight, where the ground is carpeted with soft pine needles, two figures dressed in Ninjan black, kneel opposite each other on a woven straw mat. Flower bouquets decorate the perimeter of the mat. Kamatsu, now a late middle-aged man, faces a mature Shoshone brave. Kamatsu's expression shows pride as he presents a polished black

Katana sword to the warrior. The Ninjan receives the weapon with humility and gazes at the sword with deep appreciation. He looks at Kamatsu and bows low and remarks, "Arigato Sensi! " Kamatsu bows in return and replies, "You have surpassed my expectations. You are now ready!" Kamatsu reaches into his Ninjan tunic and brings out an embroidered buckskin pouch and unfolds it to reveal a large black feather. Kamatsu's fingers clasp the quill portion and he lifts the feather up toward the sky and chants some Japanese words. The other man bows low and replies, "Chigiri Jungyo! (Pledge Obedience). The warrior raises up and Kamatsu offers the black eagle feather to him. As the man receives the symbol, his hand slightly trembles as he holds the Ninjan black feather. He is speechless and in awe at such an honour. The warrior fastens his eyes on the glossy Katana, and stares at the black feather as it glistens in the sunlight. The Ninjan bows low to his Sensi, and Otter nods and remarks, "Aho! Hai!"

CHAPTER FIVE

A New Century And A Whirl Through Time

TIME: 1880

Chief Bear Claw and a group of Shoshone braves ride their horses to the top of a high hill. The old Chief and the braves look out across the wilderness, then gaze down at a passenger train that rolls along the railroad tracks below. The Shoshone warriors watch puffs of black smoke pour out from the locomotive engine and drift into the sky above. Chief Bear Claw remarks, "The farther we ride, the more iron horse we see. Railroad tracks cover the land and cut across Buffalo hunting grounds." An aged brave next to the Chief comments, "The iron horse brings much people and many things. Everywhere the iron horse goes - White men build villages and towns. I have seen this." Chief Bear Claw looks at the seasoned brave and replies, "Our way of life is changing fast. I am afraid, soon, we will be no more!" Bear Claw's words echo in the hearts of the Shoshone braves around him and they nod their heads in agreement. The warriors on horseback gaze at the moving train below. Inside one of the passenger cars, a young girl in a frilly pink calico dress lifts her eyes off the book she's reading and looks out the window and sees Indians on the hill. The youngster tugs on her mom's arm with excitement, "Mommy look - Indians! - Real Indians!" The mother lifts her eyes toward the hill, stares a bit, then looks down at her daughter and brushes her child's hair, "Don't worry Emily, we're safe! It's different now, things are civilized!" The little girl smiles and goes back to her book, while the mother continues to look out the window. Perhaps she realizes the American Wild West will soon fade into history books, like the book she reopens - "King Arthur's Roundtable". Up a couple rows, a man sits dressed in a suit, tie and bowler hat, and holds up a newspaper to read. He turns the pages and his eyes fall on the various advertisements for new inventions; one promotes a sewing machine, another shows a telephone, and one advertisement displays a typewriter.

TIME: 1900s

The American West undergoes change far beyond the control of local and territorial residents. The days of the Pony Express, Telegraph Wire, Pioneer Wagon Trains, Overland Stage Coach, and Calvary soldiers at wooden Forts - start to change and fade away. The rugged wilderness and open prairies of Chief Bear Claw and the Shoshone braves, soon become populated with settlements and villages. Growing towns become fledgling cities bustling with inhabitants, commerce and industry. This is the age of the Industrial Revolution in America and Europe, where mechanized factories, plants and mills, turn out new products and processes using electricity. Henry Ford invents the Model T car and makes it available to people across the nation from his automotive factory in Michigan. Two brothers, Wilbur and Orville Wright, make the first successful flight of a powered airplane. Over time, flying would become a new form of travel for many people.

TIME: 1920s

This is the age known as the Roaring Twenties's. Americans in the thousands buy Henry Ford's Model T car and start to travel far and wide. Towns and cities continue to grow and expand, proving jobs and new business. People move from rural life to live and work in urban centres. Big bands are popular, and everyone wants to dance the Jitterbug. Fashion conscious men wear pin-striped suits and straw hats; while ladies favour the fancy hats and frilly dresses of the 'Flappers'. During this era, the Federal Government brings in Prohibition and outlaws alcohol production and consumption. Those wanting alcohol visit an underground club called a 'Speakeasy' and drink their booze in secret from the Police and general public. In homes across the nation, families and individuals purchase and enjoy modern inventions like - electric toasters, washing machines, vacuum cleaners, radios and television.

TIME: 1930s

The Crash of the News York Stock Market sent America into a great panic with millions of people losing millions of dollars, the economy was in ruins. What followed was the Great Depression that created a nation-wide scarcity of employment and food. Individuals and families lost pretty much everything they owned - personal savings, businesses, homes and farms. People took to moving across the country looking for work. These people camped out or stayed in shantytowns built near towns and cities. These crude ramshackle enclaves were commonly known as 'Hoovervilles', so named after President Hoover.

TIME: 1940s

The Great Depression gave way to the emergence of World War on the international stage. Japan attacked Pearl Harbour on Dec.7, 1941, causing the United States to enter World War II. Men across the nation enlisted and went off to fight overseas, and the women back home began to work in plants and factories to manufacture the equipment and supplies needed by troops abroad. Citizens at home listened to Jazz from Big Bands like Count Basie, and watched Fred Astaire dance in Hollywood movies; while over in Europe, Allied troops were serenaded by the sweet voice of Vera Lynn. The War in Europe came to an end when Germany surrendered to the Allied Forces on March 8, 1945, the Armistice became widely known as VE Day, Victory in Europe Day! Japan surrendered to America on September 2, 1945, but the official Armistice began on August 14, 1945.

TIME: 1950s

Thousands and thousands of the men return from WWII to find companies and factories strong and productive from the War Effort. The former soldiers enter the workforce and apply their military training and skills with a winning attitude. Most of the women return to domestic life and caring for family. Over time, a 'Baby Boom' sweeps the nation as men and women began to have children and start families. With companies in steady production, consumer goods available, and new family houses being built - the American life and dream was better than ever! Elvis Presley introduced the music of 'Rock-a-Billy' and became an instant star. Young people listened to popular singers were Buddy Holly, Chuck Berry, and Eddie Cochran, while older folks listened to Doris Day, Connie Francis and Perry Como. The 1950s were the carefree fun-loving days as portrayed in the TV shows, movies, and music. Overseas, America fights the Cold War against Communism, while stateside, people join the Civil Rights Movement.

TIME: 1960s

The major events of this era include the Vietnam War, the Hippie Movement, and the Assassination of President J. F. Kennedy and Dr. Martin Luther King. Young people drop out of Society and join the

Hippie movement to experiment with drugs and live a free lifestyle. America experiences the "British Music Invasion" from groups like - The Beatles, The Rolling Stones, The Who, Herman's Hermits, and The Byrds. While American 'Pop Music' includes the sounds of the Beach Boys, the Supremes, the Jackson Five, Paul Revere and the Raiders, the Temptations, and Johnny Cash. There's a Space Race between America and the Soviet Union, and America is first to land a man on the moon.

TIME: 1980s

Governor Ronald Regan of California became the 40th President of the United States. Young people listened to emerging music like New Wave and Punk, and Rock bands had 'Big Hair'. People used the Apple, Atari and Commodore personal computers on the Internet, and enjoy new technology like the Walkman, Cable Television, CVRs, video games, and music on CDs. Fashion ranged from the 'Preppie' style of golf shirt, knit sweater and pleated pants; to jean jackets, T-shirts, and faded jeans. This was the time of the Dot-Com Bubble with the sudden rise of internet companies and big stock investments. When the Bubble burst, which became known as the dot-com crash, trillions of dollars were lost and many businesses failed.

TIME: 2000s

The September 11 attack on the World Trade Towers and the US Pentagon by international terrorists will forever stand out in the America psyche. President George W. Bush was in Office when America was involved with the War on Terror and the Gulf War. There were oils spills in the environment and Hurricane Katrina battered the US Gulf States. People discovered the iPod, Google, YouTube, and Social Networking. And the increase of divorce brought changes to the traditional family unit. President Ronald Regan passed away June 5, 2004, and Barack Obama became the first black President of the Unites States on January 20, 2009.

TIME: PRESENT DAY

Desert region of the Northwest United States.

25

CHAPTER SIX

Life in a Desert Town

A popular area Roadhouse is crowded with rowdy patrons as the band rocks out with some ole' fashion Rock 'n' Roll. The dance floor is packed and people sing along as the band plays their favourite tunes. Throughout the 'watering hole' people are drinking, feasting, flirting, and some are fighting. Outside, shiny vehicles fill the Bar's parking lot - gleaming trucks, classic muscle cars, fast Imports, and luxury Sport Utility vehicles. Most of the guys and gals are inside having fun and letting off steam. Only a few people linger about in the cool night air of the desert.

An old rusted pickup with its headlights off, creeps up to the edge of the parking lot. Spike, the gang leader gives the okay and three gang members jump out of the cargo box, their shoes hit the gravel with a crunch. Tommy, the new recruit is one of them. Before them sits a glitzy new Cadillac Escalade. One of the crew pulls out a thin metal bar known as a Slim Jim, slides the bar down between the glass and the driver's door - and gives a quick pull - CLICK! The door unlocks and the kid quickly gets in and hot-wires the car - VROOM! Tommy and the other accomplice get in. A couple of men having a smoke outside, spot them and start to yell! The kid at the steering wheel floors the engine and tears out of the parking lot onto the highway. The old pickup races from behind to catch up. The men run to the road but it's too late — the thieves are gone! The stolen Escalade and the old pickup race over the desert highway for a number of miles, then turn down a forlorn dirt road, and fly over shallow hills and dips until reaching an old abandoned gas station out in the middle of nowhere. The site reminiscent of something from a cheap horror film. The Escalade and pickup pull into the back of the weathered derelict building and the engines cut. Everyone jumps out and gathers around the Escalade to admire the stolen trophy. Spike swags up and lays his arm across Tommy's shoulder and remarks with a proud grin, "Homes! That's how we carjack!" Tommy stands a bit nervous and replies, "Man, my heart is pounding!" Spike slaps the new recruit's back, "There's still more ahead, Homes!" As a couple gang members grab a old faded tarp and cover the SUV, the other members gather around their leader. One guy pipes up, "We hitting old Joe's?" Spike looks at the guy with a smirk, "Had my eye on that place for weeks. It's 'Pay Day' bro! - Let's roll." Everyone piles into the old truck, three cram the front, and two others and Tommy jump into the back. The old rust bucket fires up and tears off down the lonely dirt road.

Old Joe's Sporting Goods store is out on Canyon Road, the route that people take to get out into the outdoors where there was hunting, fishing and camping. It was a well-known location and folks from near and far shop there to get hunting rifles, fishing equipment, camping supplies and outdoor apparel. Tonight, the only sentinels guarding the place are two lampposts that cast a sodium orange glow across the storefront and parking lot. The store's neon sign is turned off and a closed sign hangs inside the front door. The Store's big windows are full of merchandise - displays of outdoor clothing, field binoculars, camouflage outfits, compound bows and arrows, fishing rods and lures, electronic fish finders, camping equipment, sleeping bags, and assorted backpacks.

The old pickup roars into the parking lot and drives behind the large cement block building and slams to an abrupt stop - the headlights slice through the small cloud of dust that wafts in the air. Three jump out of the truck cabin, and Tommy and the other two bolt out of the cargo box to land in the dirt. Spike waves his hand and they all form a quick huddle. Spike remarks, "The front door and windows have alarms. (He chuckles) The back window has nothing! The money's inside because the deposit goes to the bank in the morning." All the gang members grin and nod their heads except Tommy. The gang leader eyes the new recruit and points, "Tommy, you'll go through the back window. Once inside, you kill the alarm and unlock the front door. - This break-in is your initiation, Homes! Do it - and you're in the gang!" Tommy looks composed on the outside, but inside he's nervous and feeling hesitant, "Okay!...Got it." A gang member hands Tommy a knife and a small flashlight. He holds the knife in one hand and the flashlight in the other. They walk from the pickup to the store's back window and two guys help boast Tommy so he can reach window level. Spike instructs, "Slide the blade to trip the widow latch." Tommy looks down, all eyes are on him. He works the knife blade along the crack in the window frame until … Click!…the metal latch pops free and Tommy pushes the window open. He tosses the knife off the side to land in the dirt and turns on the flashlight to look inside. Tommy leans in and struggles to wiggle through the open window - he falls through and Tommy hits the floor inside - Thud! - Stuff scatters around, and the flashlight rolls across the cold cement floor. Spike gets below the open window, "Hey! - You okay?" Tommy replies, "Yah! I'm fine." Spike injects, "Look for the big red button - it turns off the alarm! We'll be at the front door." Tommy feels a bit bruised from hitting the cement floor and looks around and sees the beam of the flashlight. He gets up, grabs the flashlight and scans the interior and spots the alarm's blinking red button. He walks over and pressed it off - no more blinking! Meanwhile, the gang run to the store entrance and wait. Inside, Tommy walks the store's rear corridor and enters the back of the store. The light from the lamppost casts an eerie orange glow onto the store aisles and merchandise. Tommy walks up the aisle and sees Spike and crew standing outside. He unlocks and opens the front door wide. Spike the gang spill into the store and start to grab items - watches, electronics, expensive fishing reels, hi-tech equipment, guns and boxes of ammo. They pillage through the store taking anything that's worth money, then they stash the loot in the truck cargo box. Spike uses a crowbar to bust open the cash registers. He lifts out the trays full of money and dumps the contents into a canvass sack. Suddenly, there's the rumble of a big diesel engine, and a transport rig rolls into the parking lot just off the highway - brakes and idles. The gang members freeze. The trucker exits the cab and circles the rig and makes a couple hasty inspections. Satisfied, he jumps back in, fires up the cylinders and moves out and goes down the road. Tommy is rattled and turns to Spike, "That was close!" Spike grabs the canvass sack full of bills and coins, "Let's go! We got the money." Everyone piles into the pickup. The driver floors the engine and the off-road tires spray dirt as the truck spins about and roars off into the darkness. A cloud of dust wafts in the light of the lamppost. Its orange glow reveals the front door left wide open - an a baseball cap lays in the doorway.

Dave Kwan

CHAPTER SEVEN

Evidence At The Crime Scene

The Store Manager and staff at Old Joe's stand near the cash registers as Police Chief Rogers jots info on a notepad, "We need serial numbers and descriptions of what's been stolen." The Store Manager hands the Police Chief a print out, "Sure thing! Got a list of everything stolen... Ole Joe gonna have a fit!" Chief Rogers motions and an Officer next to him takes the paper. Chief Rogers finishes his scribble and comments, "Tell him, we'll catch the thieves soon - that cap gave us a lead!" The Police Chief turns and exits the front door, and the Manger and his staff prepare the store to reopen for business. Officers outside remove the yellow Police tape. After a few minutes, Police Chief Rogers and the Officers get into their squad vehicles and drive off.

At the Police Station, Officers gather in a meeting room. There's lots of chatter as the men and women await the Briefing. Chief Rogers enters through a side door and positions himself at the front of the room. He holds a pile of printouts and a ball cap and scans across the interior - and waits a few seconds for everyone's attention. The Police Chief walks over to an Officer in a front chair and hands the papers and motions for him to distribute. As the papers get passed around and Officers begin to peruse the information, Chief Rogers comments, "This looks like the same gang that hit the Liquor store in Tyler two weeks ago! Forensics has traced the tire tread, and the ball cap gives us a solid lead. This new info gets us closer...(Pause)...Now let's go get 'em!" The Officers get up and disband in teams of two. Officer Stibbs stays behind and waits until all the others are gone, then he approaches Chief Rogers, "I think I know who owns that ball cap!" The Police Chief picks up the cap to show the inside. Stibbs examines the name scrawled in felt marker on the inner lining. The Chief asks, "Ring any bell?" Officer Stibbs replies, "When I worked the Rez, there was a kid that went by that name. He did Juvie stuff - skipped school, busted windows, got drunk." The Chief grabs the cap and shakes it, "Well, if it's the same kid, he's in the big leagues now! This gang is part of the Northwest Crew that controls everything from drugs, carjacking, break-ins, to Meth labs and extortion!" Officer Stibbs takes a deep breath and replies, "I'll drive out to the Rez…see what I can find out." The Officer turns and walks toward the exit door and Chief Rogers calls out, "Be careful Stibbs! You're just another paleface with a badge." Stibbs turns about, gives a quick nod and exits the room.

The sun is high overhead and it's really hot. The kind of temperature when you look down the highway, the air weaves and ripples with waves of heat that come off the sun-baked pavement. Officer Stibbs drives the Police cruiser along the State Highway, then turns onto Indian Reservation road, and keeps driving until he sees a cluster of cinder block buildings on the horizon. Stibbs knows from his days as an Officer on the Rez that lots of local kids hang out here near the Convenience store. He steers the cruiser off the dirt road and pulls up in front of the store's shaded veranda with its cement half wall and square pillars. A group of Rez teenagers are perched on the wall drinking soda pop and smoking cigarettes. As Stibbs gets out of the Police car and puts on his western style Police Stetson, the kids watch him with wary eyes. He slowly ambles over and stands before them in the sun as they sit under the veranda's shade. The teens eye the Policeman with casual indifference. Stibbs lifts and repositions his Stetson and remarks, "Sure is hot! Any cool drinks inside?" The kids look at each other and smirk. One guy quips, "Not as hot as the Slammer!" The youths grin! Another teen pipes up, "Ya! Those cement beds get crazy hot! All the teens snicker and laugh! An older teen eyes Stibbs and asks with slight bravado, "What do you want Mr. Po-leece-man?" Stibbs gives a slight grin and glances about, "Is Desert Dawg still around?" Suddenly, the teens' faces change from prankster grins to dead-serious. The older teen replies, "No one here by that name! Sure you got the right Rez?" The kid sitting on the wall next to him remarks, "Don't know what you're talking about - Fuzz!" Officer Stibbs smiles and steps back and reposition his stance, "Well, if you happen to see Desert Dawg - let him know Stibbs dropped by." Stibbs gives a quick nod and walks back and gets into his cruiser, starts the car and drives off. The group of teens cheer and celebrate his departure.

CHAPTER EIGHT

The Long Grass House

Kathy Long Grass, Tommy's grandmother, prepares some food items in the kitchen. She's an attractive mature lady with lovely long hair and a radiant smile. Kathy exits the kitchen and approaches the dining table bringing a tray of snacks and beverages for her grandson and his two friends. Tommy remarks, "Thanks Grandma! We're starving!" As she begins to lower the tray to the table - Tommy's two friends snatch items and gobble down the goodies. A voice comes from the front door, Carl Long Grass, Tommy's grandfather, stands by the front door holding a bag of groceries; he chides, "Your friends need to remember their manners! Tommy looks at his grandpa, "They're just hungry... been really busy lately." Carl remarks in a fatherly tone,"I know you've been busy - out all night. Twice this week!" Kathy walks over and takes the bag of groceries from his arm and goes back into the kitchen. Carl steps over to the side and hangs his buckskin jacket, then walks over and sits down in an armchair. Kathy's voice beckons from the kitchen, "You boys want some more food?" The two friends glance at Tommy and shake their heads. Tommy replies back, "We're okay grandma! Thanks anyways!" A friend's cell phone BUZZES and he checks the screen. The kid blurts out, "We gotta bounce!" The other friend injects, "See ya later Homes!" The two guys get up and knuckle bump Tommy, and he comments, "Later bro!" The two guys leave the table and exit the side door they came in through. Tommy turns and glances at his grandfather. Carl looks at Tommy with a fatherly gaze, "I don't know where you got your friends. You've changed since being with them - you're different!" Tommy replies in a feisty tone, "Don't get on my case grandpa! They're the only friends I got. No one else cares about me!" Tommy gets up and retreats to his room and slams the bedroom door. Kathy stands in the archway of the kitchen with a sad expression, then steps back inside. Carl eyes the bedroom door of Tommy's room. He stands up and is about to go speak with the boy, then he pauses and slowly sits back down. He picks up the tv remote and turns on the Evening News.

In the morning, Tommy has the front seats of his car, a blue 1985 Ford Mustang, on the yard as he installs new carpet. This was his dad's old car and it's the one thing Tommy deeply cherishes. He's got tunes cranked up on the car radio as he works away. Kathy stands at the big picture window and watches her grandson outside. Carl comes up beside her and he looks out as Tommy positions and trims the auto carpeting. Kathy comments, "I know he still hurts bad — not every kid looses both parents in an accident. - The drunk driver should have got a tougher sentence - three years for taking two lives!" Kathy shakes her head as she looks at the nearby photo of their son, daughter-in-law, and eight year old Tommy. Carl takes a deep breath, "Tommy needs our love and support...now more than ever before!" Kathy turns and looks into her husband's eyes, "I'm happy he comes over for meals, but he keeps living in that old house - with his mom and dad gone, it's just cold and empty!" Carl reaches out a hand to gently clasp Kathy's shoulder and replies, "He's our grandson! We'll just have to be there for him." As his grandparents continue to watch and radio tunes blare, Tommy trims and positions the new carpet into place.

CHAPTER NINE
The Northwest Gang

Spike sits across the worn tavern table from Bossman, leader of the Northwest Gang, a big scary man with a scar down the left side of his face. Some say he got the scar in a street fight when he was a young punk, others say Bossman got it in prison during a jail yard rumble with another gang. No one knows for sure but either way, Bossman is one mean scary dude with a quick fuse. Spike looks around at the musclebound gang lieutenants sitting nearby - all tough and menacing. Bossman looks at Spike and remarks, "We need more high-end cars for overseas…(he leans forward)…You can handle that right?" Spike gives a confident yet faltering reply, "Don't worry Boss! Our numbers have grown - it's as good as done!" Bossman eyes Spike and sneers, "Anyone gives you a problem - just send word (Bossman tilts his head to crack his neck) I miss killin' people!" Spike nods compliance. Bossman gets and stands tall and imposing, "And I mean anyone… Nobody is going to stop our expansion. This territory is ours!" The big man turns and strides away and motions the gang lieutenants to follow. Alone at the back of the Bar, Spike feels nervous and takes a deep breath and chugs the rest of the beer at the bottle of the bottle.

The Northwest Gang moved into the region a number of months ago. At first it was just a few gang members - sent to scout the area and report back what they found. Then, more and more members of the gang showed up, and soon the whole territory was flooded with the Northwest Gang. The gangsters dominated the local bad boys and operated everywhere - area towns, high schools, the Indian Reservation, truck stops, ranches, and even parties. The city gang muscled out any of the local small town hoods. The Northwest Gang dealt drugs to the locals and started to rake in cash. Crew members began to boost cars, steal electronics from warehouses, set up Meth labs, and extorted businesses for protection money. The gangsters were everywhere - and everyone feared them!

At the Police Station, a Forensic Officer hands the Police Chief a file. Chief Rogers opens the folder and peruses the papers, then asks, "Prints on the ball cap match the record? You sure about it?" The Forensic Officer replies, "100 percent sure. A perfect match!" Chief Rogers taps the file folder against his right hand, looks at the man and remarks, "Time to catch a thief!" In a matter of minutes, Chief Rogers and six Officers head out the cement steps in back of the Police Station, and get into their Police cruisers. Chief Rogers is the first to pull out, then, three cruisers follow him. They drive through town and out onto the Highway toward the Indian Reservation 10 miles away. On the highway, Chief Rogers flicks on the Police Lights but doesn't put on the siren. The other Officers do the same. As people travel into town, they pass the four Police cruisers with flashing lights sand wonder what's happening. Some miles later, Chief Rogers stops at the side road to the Indian Reservation, pulls over onto the shoulder of the road and he gets out. The other Officers stop their cruisers behind the Chief's car, exit and walk up to join him. Chief Rogers turns his head and gazes at the large road sign: INDIAN RESERVATION, then looks at his Officers, and addresses them, "We're after this kid. (Shows photo) We're going to be on their land - whatever you do - don't show any disrespect. We don't want any trouble!" The Officers nod, and they return to their cars and Chief Rogers pulls out and the others follow. The Police drive onto the Reservation and go past buildings, stores, trailers, and clusters of homes. Groups of people watch the four Police cars drive by - the peoples' faces clearly show a wary curiosity and concern. The Police Chief leads the others down a dusty lane to an old weathered wooden house. The Police stop and get out.

Tommy is asleep on the sofa in the living room, the commotion and the slamming of car doors wake him up. Tommy goes to look out the window and sees the flashing lights of the Police cars and quickly turns to dash through the back of the house. Tommy flings open the back door and runs right into the arms of a Policeman. The lad struggles and yells, "Let me go! - Let me go!" Chief Rogers approaches the squirming youth and remarks, "You'll have to come with us, son. There are some questions that need answering!" An Officer holds Tommy as another Policeman reads the Miranda rights and handcuffs Tommy and put him into the back of a Police cruiser. The Police leave the property and return they way they drove. As the Police drive through the Reservation, people see Tommy in the back of the cruiser. Soon, the Police vehicles pull off Reservation land onto the highway and head toward town. Later that morning, Tommy is secured in an Interrogation Room. Tommy sits in the sculpted metal chair and drums his fingers on the metal table before him. He scans around the room - just a ceiling, floor, bare walls, and a metal door with a narrow observation window. He returns to drumming his fingers and sighs. At that moment, Police Chief Rogers opens the door and enters carrying a paper bag, and sits down opposite the youth. Tommy diverts his eyes and stares at the floor. Chief Rogers pulls out the ball cap and tosses it on the table. Tommy's eyes rivet to it. The Police Chief comments, "We know this is your ball cap, Tommy. Your fingerprints are on it, and your name is in it!" Tommy swallows and gives a glance at the Chief, "I want to go home!...I don't belong here." Chief Rogers replies in a stern tone, "I'll tell you where you belong...in jail for stealing cars and robbing stores. - That's where the bad kids go!" Tommy gets nervous and blurts, "Some gangbangers forced me to join or else!" Chief Rogers studies the teen and asks, "Where was this? Tommy replies, "A month ago...I was at Eddy's Pool Hall with some friends. Gangbangers pressured me to join. I told them no way. They beat me up bad!" Chief Rogers pulls out a pen and small notepad, "You say you were with friends? Witnesses to back up your story. Who were they?" Tommy sighs and casts his eyes to the floor, "Yah! Like they'll ever talk to you. - Fat chance of that!" The door opens and in walks Officer Stibbs. Tommy is surprised! Chief Rogers gets up and remarks, "I believe you know Officer Stibbs!" The Chief exits the room and Stibbs looks at Tommy and smiles, "Hi Tommy!" The teen is elated at seeing a familiar face, "Haven't seen you in years man! (Tommy eyes Stibbs) You look bigger - working out?" Officer Stibbs walks over and partially sits on the end of the table, and grins, "You know I believe in keeping fit!... And I also believe in helping out friends!...Tommy, I'm sorry about your dad and mom." Tommy looks at Stibbs with a puzzled expression, "How did you hear about it?" Stibbs replies, "I know the Trooper that was called to the accident. He told me." Tommy gets really quiet and a sad look covers his face, "Not the same without them, Homes!...Sometimes, I expect to see my mom cooking in the kitchen - and my dad fixing his car...But they're not there - no one's there!" Stibbs gets up and moves closer, and leans against the table near Tommy and offers solace, "Hey! I'm here for you...will help out best I can! (Pause) Your cap was found at Old Joe's. Stores have been hit all around. We traced it to one crew. - What can you tell me about them?" Tommy sits with a somber stare and replies, "Real gangbangers Homes! They claim this territory…even the Rez too. They're into everything. Real hardcore stuff. Word is out - anyone talk, your family won't walk!" Suddenly, the door opens and an Intake Officer pops his head in and looks at them both, "He goes to Lockup now!" Officer Stibbs pats Tommy on the shoulder, "Hang in there Tommy!" Officer Stibbs watches as the Intake Officer escorts Tommy out the door, down the hall and around the corner out of sight.

CHAPTER TEN

A Juvenile In District Court

The District Courthouse is an impressive structure of Georgian architecture style with wide cement steps that lead up to four white fluted Corinthian columns that identify the building's front entrance. This structure is the judicial centre of the territory where the area's legal cases are presented before the District Judge, and at times, before a Jury. It is here that Tommy's case, as well as others, will be heard and decided upon. Within the Courtroom, the space is filled with plaintiffs, defendants, prisoners, Prosecutors, lawyers, Public Defenders, families, friends, and curious spectators.

Tommy and his Public Defender sit at a polished oak table. His case is the first of the day, and the room is filled with whispers and quiet conversations as everyone waits for the proceedings to commence. Off to the side of the Courtroom, a Court Bailiff stands alert and ready. Suddenly, the side door opens and in walks Judge Spencer, a senior man with a full head of grey hair, wearing his black judicial robe. The Bailiff calls out in a loud clear voice, "All rise! Court's in session - Judge Spencer presiding!" Everyone in the Courtroom stands to their feet as Judge Spencer ascends the wood steps to the Judge's bench and sits down and puts on his wire frame reading glasses. The Bailiff announces, "All may be seated!" Judge Spencer reaches toward the stack of case dockets and picks the top one. He lays the folder before him and opens the flap and scans through the papers, then peers over his glasses at Tommy and his College-aged lawyer. Judge Spencer clears his throat - "Ahem!", then motions for the Bailiff to approach the Bench and hands him a piece of paper. The Bailiff looks at the note and stiffens up to formally remark, "The State vs Tommy Long Grass!" The Public Defender stands to his feet and tugs on Tommy's sleeve to stand up. Tommy gets off the chair and stands like a-deer-caught-in-the-headlights, he's never been inside a Courtroom and never faced a real Judge before. As the young lawyer stands attentive and professional, Tommy shifts his weight and fidgets a bit. Tommy looks at his lawyer and he gives Tommy an encouraging smile and turns his attention back to the Bench. Judge Spencer peruses over the papers, stops to glance at Tommy, then scans the file. The Magistrate adjusts his spectacles and gives a direct look at Tommy and his lawyer, flips through the docket and remarks, "Young man, you are facing some serious charges!...Grand Theft Auto, Break and Enter, Accessory to Commit a Crime, and member of a Criminal Gang." The Public Defender looks at the Judge as he extends his arm toward Tommy, "Your Honour, this teenager is genuinely remorseful and sorry for his actions and involvement. He was a naive participant, pressured to take part under the threat of bodily harm." Judge Spencer looks at the papers before him - then looks at Tommy and responds, "I will consider the fact he's a teenager of impressionable age. My concern is - will he re-offend?" The young lawyer replies, "If it please the Court, Your Honour, I'd like to have a Police Officer familiar with the boy to speak on his behalf. (Lawyer turns) We call Officer Stibbs to the stand." The Policeman gets to his feet, exits the gallery seating and makes his way to the Witness Stand and sits down. A Court Clerk approaches with a Bible and extends it level toward Stibbs. The Court Clerk comments, "Please place your right hand on the Bible and repeat after me...I promise to tell the whole truth, and nothing but the truth, so help me God!" Stibbs places his right hand on the Bible and repeats the Oath. The Clerk returns to the side area and the Judge looks directly at Stibbs and asks, "What can you tell the Court about this young lad?" Officer Stibbs turns to look at Tommy, then turns to face Judge Spencer and remarks, "Tommy lost both parents three years ago in a terrible car accident. He was thirteen at the time. Since then, Tommy has been staying in the family home - alone and unguided. He has an older brother, but he works construction and travels a lot and is seldom home. - For the most part, Tommy lives by himself!" Judge Spencer lifts his eyes off Stibbs and looks at Tommy, then the Judge scans the people in the Courtroom, the faces of many have an expression of sympathy and compassion. The Judge looks at the Policeman and asks, "Does he have any other relatives?" Stibbs replies, "He has a grandfather and grandmother - Carl and Kathy Long Grass. They live on the Indian Reservation." Judge Spencer scans the gallery, "Are the grandparents present in the Courtroom?" The Public defender quickly replies, "Yes, your Honour! The grandparents are present." Judge Spencer asks in a loud voice, "Would Tommy's grandparents please stand." Halfway in the middle on the left side, Carl and Kathy stand to their feet. The Judge looks at them and asks, "Are you Tommy's grandparents - Carl and Kathy Long Grass?" Both Carl and Kathy firmly nod in compliance, "Yes, we are!" The Judge glances at Tommy, then addresses the Courtroom, "To show the Court's mercy and compassion in providing a second chance to a young offender; Tommy will be released into your care and responsibility. Tommy would have to live at your home according to Court guidelines and restrictions... Do you accept the conditions of this arrangement?" Carl and Kathy eagerly reply, "Yes Your Honour! We accept! Tommy would be welcome to live with us." Judge Spencer removes his glasses and remarks, "Under these special circumstances, and to avoid the incarceration of a juvenile in a Federal Correctional Facility - I release Tommy Long Grass into your custody as his legal guardians, from this day forth until his twenty-first birthday when he will be of legal age." Judge Spencer pounds the gavel, Stibbs returns to his seat in the gallery. Tommy stands transfixed and his lawyer turns and puts his hand on Tommy's shoulder, "You're free to go now - under Court orders. You've got to live at your grandparents' house and be under their care and authority." Kathy and Carl rush up to hug and hold Tommy. Kathy with tears exclaims, "Let's go home!" Tommy's face shows relief. As Tommy and his grandparents make their way toward the Courtroom's exit doors, Tommy stops when he gets near Stibbs. The youth looks at the Policeman and smiles, "Thanks Homes! I owe you!" Stibbs smiles and replies, "You don't owe me anything Tommy! Just glad I was able to help.(Pause) Tommy, always remember - I'm your friend!" Tommy nods his appreciation and the trio resume their exit of the Courtroom. Tommy, Carl and Kathy go through the thick polished oak doors and enter the busy hallway and walk toward the front entrance. When they emerge onto the wide front steps of the Courthouse, Tommy, Carl and Kathy share a quick hug of celebration as they bask in the warm sunshine.

The trio descend the Courthouse steps and walk the parking lot to Carl's Chevy Malibu. Carl and Kathy get into the front seats and Tommy climbs in the back seat. The grandpa starts the engine and pulls out of the parking spot and exits the lot. At the stop sign, he signals left and steers the Malibu down Main Street that leads out of town. They pass buildings, stores and homes along the way. Tommy looks out his door window and notices town kids sprinkled here and there, hanging out in front yards and chilling at street corners. The middle class kids wear nice designer outfits. Tommy looks down at his cheap worn out clothes. Carl drives the car toward the traffic light that connects Main Street to the local Highway. He gets the red light and stops, and signals right. At the green light, the man turns the vehicle right and presses the gas pedal to reach Highway speed and heads in the direction of the Reservation. Kathy turns her head toward Tommy and remarks, "We can have bannock, fried fish and corn for supper - would you like that?" Tommy politely nods, "Sounds good grandma!" Kathy turns back toward the windshield and looks at Carl with a smile of accomplishment. Carl smiles. The Malibu goes down the Highway around curves, over hills and dips, and the long straight stretch before reaching the turnoff. Carl signals and turns right onto Reservation Road and proceeds through the Indian Reservation.

CHAPTER ELEVEN
A New Home - A New Start

Heading home, Carl and Kathy wave to folks they know. Some time later, the Malibu turns onto Plains Road and soon Carl slows down and steers into the driveway of their ranch style bungalow. At the end of the driveway beside the road is a mailbox with large letters - LONG GRASS. Arriving home, everyone exits. They leave the car and approach the cement stoop and front door. Carl uses his key to open the front door and merrily comments, "Your new home Tommy!" Tommy tilts his head and replies, "Grandpa…you know I've been here before." Standing behind, Kathy beams a big smile and places her hands on Tommy's shoulder and remarks, "You just visited before. From now on you're going to live with us!" They enter the house and Kathy goes directly to the kitchen to prepare the meal. Carl and Tommy walk over to the side hallway and Carl opens the door that Tommy sometime uses as his bedroom. Tommy stands quiet as his grandpa inspects the room, furniture, walls and ceiling. He comments, "We're gonna get you some new furniture and paint your bedroom. (He looks at Tommy) What paint colour do you want?" Tommy scans the room's interior and replies, "Something blue like the sky." Carl smiles and nods, "We can do that." Carl turns and leaves the room and Tommy sprawls out on the bed and looks up at the ceiling. The lad takes a deep breath and lays relaxed and still - the sounds of dishes being set on the table carry into the room. Kathy has set out the flatware and cutlery and laid out the bannock, fried fish and cobs of corn. The food looks appetizing. Kathy cheerfully chimes, "Supper's ready! Come and get it!" Carl gets off his favourite armchair and Tommy exits the bedroom. Everyone gets seated at the table and Kathy begins to pass around the food. Tommy scoops healthy portions onto his plate - he's really hungry. Carl and Kathy look at each other and grin. As the small family eat the meal, Carl asks Tommy, "There's something I want to talk with you about later?" Tommy is devouring his food and pauses, "What about grandpa?" The man gazes at the young lad, "Special training that would be good for you." Tommy stops chewing and takes a sip of fruit juice, he looks at his grandpa and comments, "You know I'm not good at school stuff." Carl smiles and remarks, "This type of training is not school stuff - it's different - special! It will help you in every area of your life." Tommy's interest is peeked and he stops eating and looks at his grandfather and remarks, "So grandpa, what is it?" Carl makes direct eye contact with his grandson and replies in a pleasant tone, "Martial Arts!" Tommy gives a slight chuckle as pushes his empty plate aside and comments, "You mean the Kung Fu stuff I see in movies!" Carl shakes his head, grins and replies, "No Hong Kong movie stunts - just a local Martial Arts program with a good instructor! - Interested?" Tommy sits and reflects upon what Carl just said, and he shrugs, "Hey, why not! - I'm gonna be bored living out here all the time!" Kathy and Carl smile at Tommy's reply. Kathy gets up and collects the dishes and takes them to the kitchen sink. Carl looks at Tommy, "Fine! I'll speak with my friend and mention that you'll be joining his class." Tommy gives a quick nod and gets up and goes to his room. Kathy starts to wash the plates and cutlery. Carl stands up and goes beside his wife to help dry the plates, glasses and utensils. After he's finished, he walks into the living room and over to sit down in his armchair and flips open a newspaper.

CHAPTER TWELVE
Gold Eagle Martial Arts

The Chevy Malibu drives into the one story strip plaza and stops in front of a brick building with a large glass window. Carl and Tommy exit the car and Tommy looks up at the building's overhead sign: GOLD EAGLE MARTIAL ARTS. Tommy looks through the window and sees teenagers dressed in white Martial Arts uniforms practicing moves. A man dressed in a white and black outfit stands to the side of the mat area and observes the students go through their routines. Carl puts a hand on Tommy's shoulder, "Let's go meet your Instructor." Carl pushes the front door open and he and Tommy enter inside. The Instructor looks at them, smiles and walks over. The man glances at Carl and Tommy and remarks, "Hi Carl! (Turns to Tommy) and who is this young man?" Carl puts a hand on Tommy's shoulder and gives a little squeeze and replies, "This is my grandson, Tommy. (Looks at Tommy) This is Morgan Jeffrey your Teacher - Your Sensi!" Morgan puts out his hand to welcome the young lad, "Hi Tommy! I'm glad you decided to visit us. We've just finished class - right now, the students are practicing today's lesson." Carl remarks, "Sensi, we'll keep out of the way and watch from the side." The Instructor leaves and Carl and Tommy position themselves off to the side. The Sensi maneuvers around his pupils - he corrects body position and approves proper form. After a few minutes, Morgan walks to the front of the large exercise mat and faces the class. The students stop their routines and quickly assemble in neat rows. Morgan lowers down onto both knees and the entire class does the same. Some kids are still catching their breath from the workout, while others knee quiet and composed. The Sensi looks at his students and comments, "Next month, there'll be testing for belts. I want you to practice and work hard toward your goal." The class reply in unison, "Yes Sensi!" Morgan gives an encouraging smile and remarks, "Remember - when leaving the Dojo, how we're to be at home and school - obey your parents and do your chores - and listen to your teachers and do your homework." The students heartily reply, "Yes Sensi!" The Instructor gazes across the youthful faces, "You're dismissed!" Morgan bows to the class and the students bow in return. With class over, the kids fetch gym bags, collect belongings, and get ready to leave - some walk home while some others wait for their ride. Morgan walks over to Carl and Tommy still at their spot at the side of the floor mat. Carl comments, "You got a fine group of students!" Morgan replies, "They really got heart! I train them and they work hard. (To Tommy) So Tommy, what do you think? Are you ready to join us?" Tommy shuffles his stance and answers, "Never done this stuff before." Carl leans in a bit and comments, "You'll be fine! You're a quick learner - and you're strong and healthy." Morgan adds in, "When you start - if it's difficult, I can give you extra instruction." The grandfather asks, "What do you say, Tommy? - in?" Tommy stands quiet for a few seconds as he looks around the Dojo, then nods, "Okay! I'll try it - see what happens." The Sensi responds to Tommy words, "Great! Your first class is next Wednesday. See you then!" With Tommy's decision made, Morgan leaves the two and walks to the Dojo office. Carl and Tommy exit through the front door and get into the Chevy Malibu. Carl starts the engine, reverses the car, shifts the stick and drives off. Tommy lifts his eyes to the sign overhead - GOLD EAGLE MARTIAL ARTS - He eyes the Club's Logo of an impressive flying eagle with talons extended for battle.

Somewhere in town, Spike and Crew hang out at the popular Fast Food outlets located at the outskirts of town near the highway. The outlets are busy with lots of cars and customers. Spike and gang members are hungry and grab a bite to eat. Around them are big shiny trucks, tricked out imports, expensive SUVs, rocket bikes, and family vans. As the gang chill leaning against their rides, a gangster comments, "Tommy hasn't returned my text! - Maybe he's scared." Spike sneers in reply, "He's not scared - he's a traitor, Homes! Plain avoiding us! My gut tells me he turned on us." The Homie beside Spike asks, "What are you gonna do about it?" Spike pulls out of his lean and stands up straight with a determined expression and replies, "Gonna find out where that traitor stays - gonna pay him a little visit. (punches fist into his palm) No one leaves the Northwest Crew. No one Homes!" The gang members eye each other and nod their heads in agreement.

CHAPTER THIRTEEN

Attending District High School

Carl stands outside beside Tommy's car, lays his hand on the car roof and leans down near the driver's window, "You got to be in High School - regular attendance. Court Order!" Tommy stares ahead and replies, "I'll be there!" Carl senses something is bothering his grandson and asks, "What's wrong?" Tommy raises his gaze to Carl and replies, "School and me don't work out. Hate being there!" Carls bends down to be eye level with Tommy and speaks in a fatherly tone, "Promise me that you'll be at school.(Pause) Your got your grandma and me - we'll do this together." Tommy smiles as he replies, "Okay grandpa. - I promise!" Tommy fires up the engine and drives onto the paved road toward town. Kathy watches from the home's living room window.

The District High School is an 60's construction two storey brick complex with a sizeable parking lot, and a small landscaped circle with a flag pole that flies the beloved American flag - the Stars and Stripes. The morning rush for class brings in busy school traffic - buses, parents in cars with kids, pick up trucks, family vans, and motor bikes. There's a mix of teens from around the surrounding towns, farms, and the Indian Reservation. It's a typical High School like so many across the nation with jocks, nerds, cool kids, rich kids, techies, hipsters, outcasts, and Rez kids. As students rush to class, two teachers monitor the activity from the school's elevated front steps. The majority of kids hustle to class, and some just mosey along. A few sneak off to skip school. With the last student through the door, the teachers shut the door and lock it.

Inside Tommy's new classroom, students jostle and grab desks - some are victorious and others have to settle for the desk they get. Tommy enters the classroom and spots an empty desk halfway down the left side of the room, he grabs it and sits down. In front of him sits a big jock wearing a Varsity Football jacket. Behind him is a nerd with thick glasses, and to his right sits a posh girl in designer clothes. Tommy gives a slight sigh - he's feels totally out of place. As the kids are busy chatting or on their phones, a teacher walks into the room carrying a brown leather satchel and a stack of papers. She closes the door and goes to the teacher's desk, sets down the papers and satchel, turns to grab a dry marker and begins to write her name on the whiteboard - Ms. Meagan Mills. The thirty-something lady pivots about and looks at the students and remarks, "Welcome class! My name is Ms. Mills and I'm your homeroom teacher. (Passes out papers) You gather here each morning before going off to your other classes. I'm handing out your schedule - follow it and you'll be fine! (Pause) There'll be Attendance in the morning so make sure you sign your name - otherwise, the school Office sees you as truant - missing school - then the Office will call home (looks at class) And we don't want that - right?" A couple guys poke their buddies and snicker. A prime and proper young lady at a front desk puts up her hand, "Ms. Mills?" The lady turns and looks at the student, "Yes!" The girl asks, "Do we come back here after our last class?" Megan Mills replies, "Good question! - the answer is no! Teachers take attendance at the beginning of their class. No signature means no attendance! - Makes sure you put your name down." She walks to the whiteboard that covers the room's wall behind her desk - picks up a big marker and writes in large cursive letters - American Geography - and turns to face the class. She walks over to a side rack and pulls down a large map of the American Northwest States - Washington, Oregon, Idaho, Utah, Colorado, Montana, Wyoming, and North and South Dakota. Ms. Mills announces to her students, "In class, we'll be studying these States - learning about topography, surface terrain, river systems, climate, agriculture, industry and population." A guy near the front asks, "Will we do reports?" The kids buzz at his suggestion. Meagan Mills replies, "There will be two kinds of reports: one you do on your own - and the other as part of a team." Many students begin to murmur - and a few mildly cheer. A guy on the right side of the room quips, "Do we get to pick our teams?" Ms Mills scans the group and remarks, "No! Each student will be assigned a team. - I'll pick names from a box." Now, the kids murmur and groan! A kid on the left pipes up, "What about marks?" Megan Mills pivots around to look at the entire class and replies, "50% of your mark will from class - 15% from your individual work - and 35% will be from your team report." The students take a few seconds to digest what she just mentioned - some kids sit stoic and tight-lipped, and others sit with pouty unhappy faces. SCHOOL BELL RINGS. Ms. Mills quickly injects, "See you all tomorrow!" The kids get up out of their seats and the classroom quickly empties as kids rush off to another class. There's some chatter as a few kids check their Schedule for room numbers and classroom location. The school halls get crowded.

The school day comes to a close and everybody leaves in assorted vehicles - buses, cars, bikes and vans. Tommy hustles to his blue Mustang and cranks the engine - VROOM! He pulls out of the parking lot and heads toward the highway. Tommy motors past gas stations, strip plazas, stores and bars. People are out and about - workers getting off shift, parents picking up kids at school, families buying groceries and running errands. The lad takes it all in. Tommy cruises along until he approaches the Reservation Road exit. He turns and heads along the main artery. The buildings on the Rez are hit and miss - some businesses are well-to-do, while others are in need of maintenance and repair. Tommy watches as his Native American people do the same as the townies - get off work, buy supplies, taxi kids from school, and get groceries. He signals and turns the wheel onto Plains Road that will take him home. He navigates the bends, dips, curves and straight stretch before reaching the house. He steers into the driveway and parks the car beside the large tree on the property. Tommy cuts the engine. Kathy stands in the doorway with the front door open and calls out. "Tommy! Can you please help?" Tommy replies, "Ok grandma! Be right there." Tommy exits and shuts the car door and hurries up the front steps and into the house. Inside the living room, Kathy is standing next to a large mirror with ornate antique trim. His grandmother beams and mentions, "I picked it up at a garage sale. Beautiful - isn't it?" Tommy walks over and checks out the mirror, "Looks pretty cool! (Inspects details) How's you get it here?" Kathy proudly grins, "The lady and her brother drove it out here. He carried it in but didn't have time to help hang it." Tommy bends and picks up the mirror with a hand grip on each side, "I'll lift this and you can show me where you want to hang it." With Tommy lugging the mirror, Kathy steps back to stand in the centre of the room and scans around the living space, looking here and there. The mirror is getting heavy, even for a strapping young teen, and Tommy remarks, "Grandma, you find a spot yet? This mirror is getting heavy!" Kathy's eyes light up as she points to her designated place and chimes, "There

- Perfect!" Tommy carries the mirror over to the wall and Kathy gets a measuring tape and locates the correct spot and height. She pencils a mark and pounds in the anchor hook - then steps back. Tommy lifts the mirror to the proper level and attempts to latch the back wire onto the hook. After three attempts, the wire finally catches and the mirror hangs secure. He steps back and joins Kathy. They both eye-ball the new piece of home decor. Kathy steps forward and grabs the frame to correct the tilt until the mirror sits level and true. Tommy remarks, "Looks good grandma!" Kathy beams a contented smile and replies, "Yes it does! (To Tommy) Thanks Tommy, couldn't have done this without you!" Tommy steps closer and preens himself, "Glad to help grandma!" Kathy looks at her grandson, "Supper soon! Fried chicken and macaroni salad." Tommy grins and remarks, "Great! - I'm staving!" Kathy walks into the kitchen and Tommy goes into his room, tosses his backpack in the corner and flakes out on the bed - and stares at a Martial Arts poster.

CHAPTER FOURTEEN
Making New Friends

Officer Stibbs and Tommy are spending some catch-up time at a local Ice Cream Parlour, each enjoying a double scoop cone. This is a 'buddy time' for the two friends as they reconnect after not seeing each other for a while. Officer Stibbs and Tommy joke, laugh, and carry on with fun silly antics. Tommy takes a bite of his Chocolate Blast and comments, "It's sure good to see you, Homes!" The Policeman looks at the teenager, "I wanted to know if things are working out?" Tommy smiles and replies, "Grandpa and grandma treat me real good - I even joined a Martial Arts class - gonna start soon!" Stibbs takes care of some dripping ice cream on his cone and remarks, "That's good, Tommy! What about school? You doing okay?" Tommy adjusts his stance on the sidewalk and leans against the street light and replies, "School is school - but this time it seems different." Stibbs perks up, "Different - How?" The teenager licks his ice cream and gives his reply, "This time, I find the stuff interesting - not bored like before." His Policeman friend puts out his hand and messes up Tommy's hair, "Sounds to me like you got the attitude of a winner!" Tommy laughs and remarks, "At least I ate my cone first!" Tommy reaches out and tries to grab his friend's Police hat. Stibbs laughs as he fends off the playful attack.

Later on, Wednesday evening, Tommy wears his white Martial Arts uniform and stands in a row with other students - attentive and ready for instruction. Sensi Jeffrey assumes a fight position before the class of eager teens, and announces, "Today, we will learn the Dragon Fist technique to disable an attacker. Pair up and take positions." The students quickly pick partners and find floor space. First timer Tommy doesn't know anyone much less what to do. He stands between two students, a tall kid named Connor to his left, and a girl named Sarah who is shorter than him that stands to his right. Sarah turns to Tommy with a smile, "You're new here, so I'll be your partner - if that's okay with you?" Tommy glances around at the matched up pairs and replies, "That's okay! I don't know what to do anyways." Connor pipes up, "She's tough dude!(Chuckles) You'll be sorry." Sarah gives a rebuttal, "Never mind Connor! He razes all the newbies (to Tommy) The Sensi demonstrates the new technique. We form pairs and practice our moves." Tommy looks at her and quips, "Does it matter if I'm bigger than you?" Connor overhears and snickers! Sarah smiles and remarks, "Don't worry about that!" With the class teamed up, all eyes focus on Sensi Jeffrey. He moves and fixes his body to illustrate correct position for the legs and arms, then he strikes forward with the Dragon Fist. The Sensi comments, "The Dragon Fist increases your force upon an opponent. - Hit the centre of the stomach at the diaphragm, it delivers a powerful punch and knocks the wind out of your attacker! Watch me again (Demonstrates) Now, practice with your partner. One will deliver the punch - the other will block. Later, you can switch." Sensi Jeffrey rehearses the maneuver more slowly and all the students keenly watch his arm position and fist formation. When he finishes, he motions for the class to begin their practice. Tommy observes Sarah and notes her stance and limb position. Tommy checks his foot placement - then looks at Sarah. She asks, "You feel ready? Tommy nods and replies, "Think so!" Tommy no sooner got his words out when Sarah strikes with blistering speed - and stops. Tommy never even got to move. He looks down at her fist a quarter inch from his stomach midsection. Sarah comments, "You didn't protect yourself." Tommy replies, "How could I , you were so fast!" Sensi Jeffrey walks up, smiles at the two and comments, "Tommy, I see you got yourself a good partner. Sarah is one of our top students. She wins Competitions every year!" He points his arm and Tommy glances over at the Trophy wall lined with Awards. Tommy grins and replies, "Guess size doesn't matter." Sensi Morgan puts his gaze on the young lad and comments, "Size is just one factor. Martial Arts teaches you Offence and Defence - how to use your opponent's size and strength to your advantage. We teach you ways to protect yourself, and how to stop an attacker." Tommy glances over to Sarah, "Well - all I know is Sarah's fast and got the drop on me." The young lady encourages, "You'll be able to do what I can once you learn." Morgan Jeffrey remarks, "Look around Tommy (sweeps arm across the room) Every student started where you are today - and in time, you'll be able to do martial Arts like them." The Instructor gives Tommy an encouraging pat on the shoulder and resumes his tour of the other students. Sarah gets Tommy's attention, "See my fighting stance. Notice how I form my fist. Look at my strike position." Tommy observes all that Sarah mentioned. He copies her exactly and responds, "I think I got it now!" Sarah remarks, "Good! Now, attack me!" Tommy lunges forward and Sarah blocks. Tommy repeats again and again, each time Sarah deflects his punch. Tommy pauses - refocuses. Sarah holds position. Suddenly, Tommy strikes with speed and force - and hits Sarah in the stomach - Sarah buckles. Tommy stops and blurts, "I'm sorry Sarah! I didn't mean to hit you." Sarah straightens up and grins, It's okay Tommy! You got past my block - you did good. Real good!" Tommy's face lights up at Sarah's comment. As they continue in the practice, Tommy's expression begins to show more confidence as he and Sarah spar. Toward the end of class, Sensi Jeffrey takes his place at the front of the mat. All the students stop working out and assemble in rows. Tommy stands beside Sarah, he's breathing heavy from the workout. He proudly smiles. The Instructor and the students all lower to their knees. Sensi Jeffrey remarks, "Please remember our Dojo Motto - At home, at school, anywhere - Be your best! Do your best!" All the students in unison reply, "Yes Sensi!" Sensi Jeffrey glances over at Tommy and gives an encouraging smile, then he looks across the neatly formed rows of students and bows to them. The entire class bow in return. With instruction over, the kids get their backpacks, duffle bags and belongings, and head off. Some get on their bicycles and motor bikes, while others wait for rides from parents. Tommy heads toward the exit. As he walks past Sarah, she comments, "I was happy to be your partner today! You did really well for your first time!" Tommy looks at the gal, "Thanks Sarah! I learned a lot from you - You're good!" She replies, "So maybe next time we can buddy up again?" Tommy ponders a few seconds and remarks, "Yah! I'd like that. - See you." Tommy goes out the front entrance toward his Mustang, and Sarah stands with a gleam in her eye.

Next week at suppertime, Carl and Kathy treat Tommy to dining out at a popular local eatery. They enter the establishment's front doors and see the restaurant is busy with patrons having meals. Waitresses carry plates of food and line cooks put up orders ready to be served. Carl, Kathy and Tommy look over the crowd and spot an empty table midway in the restaurant. Carl leads the way through the tables - then he abruptly stops. There at a table before him sit Morgan Jeffrey, Steve

Armstrong, Barry Osprey and Eli Waters having their meal. The men stop eating and look up at Carl - who is quickly joined by Kathy and Tommy. Carl remarks, "Hi guys! How's it going?" Morgan replies with a grin, "The roast beef is excellent!" Carl puts a hand on Tommy's shoulder and comments, "Tommy, you know your Sensi, Morgan Jeffrey (Tommy nods). Let me introduce these other men to you. (He points) Steve Armstrong is a welder, Barry Osprey is an Auto Mechanic, and Eli Waters runs a horse ranch." Tommy speaks out, "Pleased to meet you!" The three men smile and give the lad a friendly nod. Carl injects, "Well, better let you guys get back to your food. (Grins) I know you all got big appetites." Morgan playfully waves Carl to move along. Kathy, Tommy and Carl reach their table and get seated. A cheerful waitress comes up and gives each a menu - then pulls out her pen and order pad.

A few days pass and Tommy is about to enter his High School Homeroom. Megan Mills sits at her desk as the students pour into class. It's a moment of organized confusion as kids bump into each other to grab their seats. Tommy is the last one through the door, and Ms. Mills asks, "Tommy, please close the door." Tommy turns and shuts the door and walks to his desk. One of the big jocks sticks out his foot and trips Tommy. His books and notebook go flying as Tommy stumbles. The class breaks out laughing! Ms. Mills scolds, "Students - that's not funny!" A kid in the back snickers and mumbles, "Oh yes it is!" Tommy regains his poise and picks up his books and notebook - gives a cut-eye to the culprit, moves to his desk and sits down. A student on the far right of the room remarks, "Miss Mills. I lost my homework - almost finished the assignment too!" Some of the guys make sad faces and wipe their eyes with boo-hoo tears. Megan Mills asks, "Where did you put it last?" The youth replies, I put it on the kitchen counter but it disappeared!" Ms. Mills looks at her class and suggests, "Will someone in class be willing to share their assignment notes?" The teacher looks around - no student seems interested - then Tommy puts up his hand, and comments, "My notes aren't the best, but he's welcome to them!" Megan Mills nods her head with a smile, "Good! Now that that's settled - let's open our textbooks to Topography and Physical Features."

As the students are in class, outside the school at the back of the football bleachers, a gangster called Griffin holds a clear plastic bag with coloured pills. The tough guy chides, "If you want the full dose - then pay the full price!" The four students rummage through their pockets and count out their money. One kid collects the bills and hands the cash to Griffin and comments, "There! Should be enough bro." The student standing next him is edgy, "Hurry up! - Before a teacher sees us." Griffin grabs and counts the bills, then offers the bag of contraband. One kid takes it and nervously stuffs the plastic bag into his pants. Griffin steps forward and puts his face inches from one student, and threatens, "Get this! - I'm not your bro!" The students sheepishly slink back, turn and race toward the school building. Griffin smirks and pulls out a big wad of bills and adds in the new money. He strides over to his muscle car, cranks the engine and presses the gas pedal - DEEP ROAR - then peels away.

CHAPTER FIFTEEN

Spike and Crew Come Calling

Carl, Kathy and Tommy are in the living room when they hear - VROOM! VROOM! VROOM! They quickly go to the big picture window, move the curtains aside and see three cars with tinted glass pull into the driveway and stop. The cars shimmer and shake as the powerful engines idle and rumble. Next, the car horns blare loud and hold......H-O-N-K!! The first car's driver window rolls down and Spike sticks his head out and yells, "Tommy! Tommy! Come out Homes - your old crew is here!" Tommy stands with Kathy and Carl at the picture window and looks out at his former gang. Suddenly, Carl disappears from view. Spike and the gang laugh as they repeatedly honk their car horns. Carl opens the front door and steps out onto the cement stoop. The horns abruptly stop. Carl raises his voice in a firm tone, "Tommy's not coming out! He won't be running around with you anymore!" Spike looks at his gang members and gets mad and steps out of the car. The other car doors open and the entire gang get out of their cars. Carl looks and sizes up things - eleven young toughs standing macho! Carl steps off the stoop and moves to the middle of the large front lawn. With his crew in tow, Spike swags over and confronts the older man. The gangsters spread out to surround Carl. They hold knives, crowbars and lead pipes, and move their weapons in a threatening manner. Carl turns to look at the living room window, Kathy is on her cell phone and Tommy is frozen just starring. Spike barks at Carl, "Look old man! Tommy is one of us - once you're in - you don't get out!" (Spike Yells) NO ONE GETS OUT!" Carl gives the young punk a steely stare and replies, "I'm telling you and your gang to get off my property - NOW!" Spike turns to his crew, smirks, then suddenly lunges at the grandfather - Carl grabs Spike's arm and flips him hard face-first into the ground. Spike scrambles back up - with bruises and a bloody nose. The young thug embarrassed and hurt, cries out, "Get the old man! Beat him up!" The angry gang members around Carl begin to swing and move their knives, pipes and crowbars to and fro - then rush in. Carl lets loose knockout kicks, powerful punches, disabling blocks and lightning strikes. The old man decimates the young toughs and renders them knocked unconscious, doubled-over, and reeling in pain with broken noses, broken bones - and broken pride! The gangsters limp and carry themselves back to their cars. Spike stands livid and scowls holding his twisted arm, and yells out a threat, "Nobody does that to us and lives! Hear me old man - you're a dead man! A dead man - you got that!" The defeated gang leader gets into his vehicle and all three cars fire up their engines and tear off the property. They floor it down the road and outta sight. The front door opens and Kathy and Tommy race to Carl's side. He has a cut on his arm and shoulder, and a scrap across his forehead. Kathy looks at Carl's wounds and remarks, "I called the Police! They should be here any minute." Just as she finishes speaking, SIRENS approach. Three squad cars and a Paramedic van pull onto the grounds. Officers quickly exit and the Reservation Police Chief comes over to them. He scans the trio and comments, "We radioed to set up road blocks - they won't get far! (Checks Carl) Better get you looked at!" The Police Chief motions a Paramedic over and he starts to check things out. Carl shows his arm and comments, "Just a small cut - a few stitches." The Paramedic ushers Carl to the back of the ambulance and Carl parks himself on the edge of the interior. The Paramedic cleans and dresses the wound, and remarks, "Good thing the cut wasn't deeper - otherwise a severed artery!" Kathy and Tommy walk up to Carl, he looks at them, raises his arm to show the stitches and remarks, "Hey look - a battle scar!" Kathy rolls her eyes and Tommy is partially still in shock, then he asks excitedly, "Grandpa - how'd you do it? - I mean - take on all those guys at once?" The grandfather gazes at his grandson and replies, "When I was your age, someone taught me Martial Arts. This time, I used it for Self Defence!" Tommy is pumped, "Wow grandpa! I had no idea!(Pause) Will I be able to fight like that?" Carl remarks, "First things first! - Stick with your Martial Arts training!" Tommy gives some quick Karate chops, "I'm ready man!" Carl smiles and he reaches out and messes Tommy's hair, "All in good time!" Carl gets off the back of the ambulance, and the three walk past Officers collecting discarded weapons and other evidence. They go up the front steps and into the house.

CHAPTER SIXTEEN

The Northwest Gang Intimidate

Out in the rugged desert region, inside an old industrial auto yard warehouse, boisterous gangsters gather in a big circle. It's sparring time! In the middle, Bossman faces five enormous thugs. Bossman has jeans and no shirt - his body ripped with muscle and covered with tattoos. The five opponents are wielding chains, clubs and knives. Bossman assumes a Martial Art fighting stance as he eyes the five attackers. Suddenly one thug swings a metal club while another swipes his knife blade. Bossman kicks the knife away then pivots with a roundhouse to KO the guy, then he blocks and grabs the club and repeatedly smashes the club against the attacker's head putting him down. The other three close in to attack - Bossman spins about with his heavy boot and kicks two unconscious - they drop to the cement floor. Bossman grabs the last thug and pummels him in a flurry of blows - then tosses his motionless body aside. Bossman looks at his defeated attackers unconscious and withering on the floor and he lifts both arms high in victory. The gangsters around him CHEER! They break out chanting the name of their leader, "Bossman! Bossman! Bossman!" Bossman smiles wide and thoroughly revels in the adulation and attention.

CAR HORNS SOUND!

Spike and his crew roll into the large auto yard littered with assorted stolen vehicles. Armed Northwest Gang members and Lieutenants give cold stares. Spike exits the car nursing his sprained arm and calls out to a nearby Lieutenant, "I need to see Bossman!" The gangster leader waves to a thug by a door and he runs inside. Soon word spreads.

LOUD MECHANICAL NOISE.

Two large industrial steel doors split apart - and out strides Bossman and a group of musclebound thugs. Spike and his crew stand tense and nervous. The gruff gang leader swags up to Spike and gets in his face, "What you doin' Homes? Don't you have cars to jack!" Spike is tiffed about their recent defeat and belly-aches, "We got trouble! - Big trouble!" Bossman steps back, tilts his head and eyes Spike and the gang, "What kind of trouble?" Spike remarks in a shaky voice, "A home boy cut out on us - stays with his grandparents. We went to get our soldier - but his grandfather stopped us!" Bossman is stunned and gets wide-eyed, he can hardly believe his ears, "Stopped you!?...... Stopped your whole crew!" Spike is totally embarrassed and replies, "He's a tough old man! - Knows that Karate stuff!" Bossman scans the local crew and bellows, "Karate! Tough guy! - Where's this guy live?" Spike remarks, "Some old Indian on the Reservation! He lives on Plains Road - the mailbox says Long Grass!" Bossman motions to a lieutenant and whispers in the thug's ear. The gangster nods and quickly rounds up some other thugs and they depart with haste. Bossman turns to Spike and crew, then orders, "You and your crew get back to business - we need those cars! - I'm gonna send this tough guy a message!" Bossman pivots about and heads back into the big warehouse with his posse following. Spike and his crew climb into their cars and tear out of the auto yard toward town.

The next day, Carl comes out of the hardware store carrying a gallon of paint and some brushes and rollers. As he walks to the Malibu he notices a black sedan with darken windows parked to the far side. The sedan looks out of place in the store's parking lot. Carl loads the supplies into the car trunk and gets behind the wheel and starts the Malibu. The black sedan's big engine also fires up! DEEP RUMBLE! As Carl pulls away, he notices the black sedan starts to follow him. He drives out of the parking lot, down the street and around town a bit - the black sedan follows at a distance. Carl takes the street out of town and turns onto the Highway and speeds up on a straight stretch, the black sedan also speeds up to follow and keep pace. Carl glances in the review mirror, the sedan's opaque windows limit him from knowing who's inside that car. He looks down the road and floors the Malibu and races down the straight stretch and the other car does the same. Carl suddenly brakes and stops on the Highway and he glances in the side mirror, the black sedan is also stopped and hangs back at a distance with its powerful engine rumbling. Out in the middle of nowhere, the two cars just stop and idle, surrounded by desert sand and cactus. It all seems odd and somewhat threatening. Carl is just about to exit his car when he hears the black sedan's tires squeal, and looks in the rearview mirror to see the sedan turn around and race off toward town. Carl takes a sigh of relief - then a pondering expression comes over his face. He shifts into drive and goes toward the Reservation.

Kathy just got her hair done at her favourite Salon. She stands at the cash register and pays the stylist and leaves her a generous tip. Kathy exits the front door and stands on the sidewalk. She watches as a black sedan with dark windows pass by her ever-so-slowly. It gives her the creeps and she shutters. Kathy turns and walks down the sidewalk and gets into her car parked by the curb. She starts the engine and signals to merge with the traffic. An off-road pickup stops to let her into traffic, Kathy waves thanks to the young couple in the truck's front seat as she leaves the curb. As she drives down the street and goes through an intersection, Kathy notices the black sedan pull out from a side street and get behind her a few cars back. She changes lane and the black sedan changes lane. Kathy turns left onto another street and the black sedan turns and keeps tailing her. Now, Kathy begins to feel stressed and afraid. Her forehead begins to get moist from some slight perspiration, her heart beats faster. As Kathy drives along the street she sees a plaza up ahead on her right and notices a Police cruiser in the parking lot. She cranks the wheel and zooms into the parking lot and pulls into a spot near the Police cruiser and cuts the engine. Kathy looks out at the street to watch the creepy black sedan drive by and keep going. Kathy takes a deep breath and glances down - her hands are trembling!

Later that evening at their house on Plains Road; Carl, Kathy and Tommy are dining on baked salmon, home fries, green peas, corn, and garden salad. Carl and Kathy are both more quiet than usual. Kathy looks at her husband, "Honey, you see lost in thought - anything wrong?" Carl comes to life and shifts his gaze to Kathy and replies, "No Dear - I'm good! Just thinking how to fix Tommy's room. (Smiles) Want to make it A-Class!" Tommy shovels more fries onto his plate and remarks, "Grandpa, I'm okay with it now! You don't have to do anything special for me." The grandfather looks at his grandson with fondness, "To your grandma and me - you are special! That's why we want to give you the best room we can." Kathy leans over and gives Carl a kiss on the cheek, smiles and comments, "Who's ready for some Blueberry pie with French Vanilla ice cream?" Tommy and Carl's eyes light up. Kathy gets up from the table and goes into the kitchen and returns with a flaky golden crust delicious Blueberry pie and a quart of vanilla ice cream. She cuts and dishes out the dessert and tops each serving with generous vanilla scoops. Tommy and Carl take the helping with eager delight. Kathy serves herself a modest portion. All three savour their yummy dessert! As they eat, Carl clears the throat, and pauses to comment, "It seemed some car was following me today!" Tommy stops his spoon halfway and looks at his grandpa. Kathy puts down her fork, looks directly at Carl and remarks in an alarmed tone, "There was a car that followed me today too! A creepy black car with dark windows. It kept following me everywhere I went - ever since I left the Beauty Salon." Carl quickly injects, "That's the car that followed me! A black sedan with tinted windows!" Kathy and Carl look at each other. Tommy remarks, "In the gang, I remember hearing about a black car with really dark windows - it belonged to a gang leader." Kathy with a worried expression reaches out to clutch Carl's hand, "Honey, what are we going to do?" Carl cups her hand with his and replies, "Darling, things will be okay! I'll let the Police know what happened. Officers will keep a close watch on the car. If anything - the Police will nab them in a heartbeat!" Kathy feels more relaxed after Carl's assurance and she smiles relief. Tommy looks at his grandparents, then turns away and stares in silence.

CHAPTER SEVENTEEN
Tommy At Martial Arts

Sensi Jeffrey observes how Tommy has developed his ability and skill in the Martial Arts class. The Instructor closely watches as Tommy correctly performs the Katas and fight techniques. During the session, Tommy spars with a fellow student - and wins! Sensi Jeffrey walks over to Tommy and comments, "You're showing real improvement! Keep up the good work." The teenager replies with a determined nod, "Thank you Sensi! I try to practice every moment I get." The Instructor moves to the front of the exercise mats and addresses all the students, "Regionals are in two months. We are allowed five entries. If you want to compete - please let em know!" The class get excited at the news and chatter fills the room. Sarah looks at Tommy and asks, "Tommy, why don't you enter?" Tommy waves his hand and shakes his head, "Sheesh - No way! I'm just a beginner." Sarah encourages her buddy, "It's an open Competition for all Dojos - even new students can enter." Tommy glances around the room to point and remark, "There're guys better than me. I wouldn't stand a chance!" Sarah steps closer and looks Tommy in the eye, "Remember, it's not about size or strength, it's about how good you are - and Tommy, you're good!" Tommy stands quiet and reflects on what Sarah said. Just at that moment, Sensi Jeffrey comes over to them both and gives his insight, "Tommy - I think you should enter Regionals. It would be a great experience and I believe you'd win!" The young man is gobsmacked at his Teacher's comment. He glances at Sarah and Sensi Jeffrey and replies, "Ok! I will do it! Go to Regionals." The Instructor and Sarah smile their approval at Tommy's decision.

TWO MONTHS LATER...

Martial Arts competitors, family, friends and spectators, fill the well-lit modern auditorium. Various Martial Arts Clubs and Sensis wear their coloured Dojo outfits. Tournament Judges are seated behind a long table situated on an elevated platform, enabling the Judges to see the Contestants and the entire Tournament floor. Sensi Jeffrey and the Gold Eagle Dojo members are gathered in the assigned zone at the mat's side. All the Dojos line the mat's perimeter. Everyone is excited! There's a CLICK and an electric HUM fills the auditorium - then an announcer's voice comes over the PA system, "Welcome everyone to our Regional Martial Arts Tournament! Our Competition will commence at 9:00 am. (All eyes on the wall clock) Sensis, please have your students ready for their scheduled bouts. - Thank You!" The microphone clicks off. Tommy, Sarah and the others look at Sensi Jeffrey as he peruses the Tournament Schedule printout. Morgan Jeffrey announces to the kids, "Sarah, you compete at 9:15 and Connor is at 9:30 am (Scans sheet) and Tommy, you go on the mat at 10 am. The others are in the afternoon." The kids buzz among themselves. Tommy stares out at the large open mat area and comments, "Such a big space - so wide and open!" Sarah leans in and remarks, "Has to be big so we can fight and move. It also let's the Judges clearly see what we do." Tommy turns his gaze toward Sarah, "Sparring in our Dojo is one thing - fighting a stranger in front of everybody is something else!" Sarah gives Tommy's arm a friendly squeeze and she tries lift his confidence, "You'll do fine! Just remember what you've been practicing." Tommy grins sheepishly. Sensi Jeffrey comes over, "Tommy, remember your routines! Watch your opponent's hands, feet and eyes, - especially the eyes! They tell you when a move is coming." Tommy repeats, "Watch the eyes!" Sarah smiles and remarks, "Yes! Watch the eyes."

AUDITORIUM BUZZER!

The first two contestants, one in a blue outfit, the other wearing a red outfit, walk out onto the centre of the mat and stop. They both turn to face the Judge's table and bow respect. Next, they turn and bow to each other, then step back and stand alert. RINGSIDE BELL! Quickly, both contestants take a fighting stance and eye each other. The red contender unleashes a roundhouse kick and the blue contestant swiftly ducks and backs up. The red fighter attacks with punches - the blue fighter blocks and strikes the red opponent with a solid blow. A voice over the PA announces, "2 points. Blue." The two fighters back off to regain position. The blue opponent quickly drops to sweep his leg and knocks the red fighter off balance. The blue fighter grabs his opponent in a chokehold - the red contender breaks the grip and powerfully flips the blue fighter onto the mat. THUD! The voice on the PA speaks, "2 points. Red" 1 MINUTE WARNING BELL. With just one minute remaining to defeat your opponent, both fighters blitz. The red guy throws a punch and the blue guy blocks. The blue fighter kicks and it's blocked by his red opponent. There's a flurry of strikes and blocks. Both fighters keep up the intense battle. TOURNAMENT BUZZER. The audience cheer and applaud the competitors. A Referee steps between the two contestants, both are sweating and breathing heavy and stand with anticipation. The Referee and the two fighters watch the Judges' table and await the outcome. Tommy turns to his Sensi, "Who won?" Morgan Jeffrey comments, "It's a close one! Let's see what the Judges decide." There's a momentary lull across the crowded auditorium. Everyone watches as the Judges confer in whispered conversation. The blue contestant and the red contestant eye each other as perspiration runs down their face. A slim older man with grey hair and beard steps up to the microphone at the Judges' table, he looks at the two fighters and remarks, "The Tournament winner is Blue!" Loud applause fills the interior. Both fighters shake hands and exit the mat to their Dojo section. The blue contender walks with his arms raised in victory. Sensi Jeffrey looks at the Schedule and remarks, "Sarah, you're up next!" Sarah checks her Gold Eagle outfit and replies, "Ready Sensi!"

AUDITORIUM BUZZER

Sarah ascends the mat and moves to the centre. Her gold outfit gleams under the Tournament lights. From the opposite side strides a large teenage guy in green attire. The two combatants face the Judges and bow, then face each other and bow. RINGSIDE BELL. The green opponent unleashes a front kick and Sarah steps aside - grabs his ankle and flips the guy backwards onto the mat. THUD! The PA system announces, "2 points. Gold" The green fighter springs to his feet and sends out a barrage of punches which Sarah deftly blocks and deflects. She quickly spins with a roundhouse that blasts her opponent off his feet and onto the floor. In his excitement Tommy yells, "Way to go Sarah!" The Announcer's voice fills the interior, "3 points. Gold." The green opponent spins and twirls to his feet and runs at Sarah - jumps to flip and kick Sarah in her back shoulder area to knock her off-balance. The fellow's Sensi pumps his fist and yells, "Yes!" The PA system carries the score, "3 Points. Green." ! MINUTE WARNING BELL. The green contender forcefully grabs Sarah to execute a chokehold - but Sarah squirms free. He reaches out and grabs her collar and she ducks her head, spins her body around and kicks him hard in the stomach. The guy crumples to the mat with a contorted face. AUDITORIUM BUZZER. The Referee walks to the mat's centre stage. Sarah is on his left and the green opponent in on the Referee's right. Sarah stands calm while the big guy grimaces in pain. All eyes are on the Judges as they compare scores and talk in muffled tones. One Official leans into the mic to announce, "Tournament Winner is Gold!" Sensi Jeffrey, Tommy and the Gold Eagle members erupt with cheers and high fives! Sarah turns to shake her opponent's hand - and he slights her and walks away unhappy. She looks over to Sensi Jeffrey and he tilts his head and shrugs his shoulders. Sarah walks off the mat and Sensi Jeffrey, Tommy and the teammates congratulate her. Tommy looks at Sarah and with a big grin, "Awesome! You were totally awesome!" Sarah takes a breath and replies, "Thanks Tommy! The two place themselves at the mat's edge and watch Connor get into position on the Tournament floor. Before Connor, stands a girl with a ponytail wearing a purple outfit. They bow to the Judges's table, then bow to each other and step back into a fight position. RINGSIDE BELL. Connor and the girl circle around to size each other up. Connor moves in to strike but the girl ducks the punch. She swiftly spins around to hit Connor's chin with her elbow - it knocks Connor backwards. The PA announcer informs the score, "2 points. Purple." Connor recovers and grabs the girl's sleeve and throws her hard to the floor. THUD! She's nearly knocked out and slowly gets to her feet. The announcer voices, "3 points. Gold." Connor eyes his opponent and quietly remarks, "That'll teach you!" The female fighter gives a hard look and with lightning speed unleashes a flurry of kicks and punches that Connor cannot block - she strikes Connor repeatedly! The Announcer exclaims, " 3 Points. Purple." AUDITORIUM BUZZER. Both fighters lock eyes in a fierce gaze. The Referee comes into the centre of the two contestants and all three face the Judges. The Officials huddle and speak with muffled voices - then a lady Judge speaks into the microphone, "Tournament Winner is Purple!" Connor and the girl face each other and shake hands in sportsmanship spirit, as they shake hands the girl gives Connor a haughty smirk. They both walk off to their Dojo areas. Connor exits the mat and looks at Morgan Jeffrey. The Sensi comments, "Don't worry losing Connor! There's another Competition in the Fall." Connor is upset, "I could have beat her! Next time, I'll be prepared." Sarah, Tommy and others gather around Connor to lift his spirit. Sarah comments, That was a good throw! Textbook move." Connor looks at

Sarah and replies, "I learned that from you. Remember, you gave me pointers last year?" Sarah nods. Tommy watches their exchange and gets worried. Sensi Jeffrey puts his arm on Tommy's shoulder and encourages, "You're ready for this - just watch their hands, feet and eyes." The first-timer mutters, "Especially the eyes!" Tommy manages a faint smile and turns toward the Tournament mat. Pumped and nervous, Tommy repeatedly clenches his fists. The Gold Eagle teammates stand near him.

AUDITORIUM BUZZER

Tommy ascends the mat and walks toward the middle - there's a thick spongy feel to his feet, the mat surface is tactile yet cushioned. He reaches the centre. From the other side walks a young man dressed in a black outfit with an embroidered dragon crest on the front. The opponent approaches with confidence and stops a few feet away. On cue, both young men turn and bow to the Judges and then bow to each other. They both step back and assume a fighting stance. RINGSIDE BELL. Suddenly, Tommy's opponent sends out a straight arm punch. Tommy turns his torso and deflects with a block. The opponent swings his other arm and Tommy stops the strike. Both contenders back up and reposition. The PA system informs, "2 points. Gold." The opponent quickly pivots and kicks Tommy's side. Sensi Jeffrey yells out, "Watch his feet Tommy!" The Announcer speaks into the mic, "3 points. Black." Tommy and his opponent circle each other eager for battle. Tommy notices his opponent's eyes blink before he goes to punch or kick. Tommy braces himself. Sure enough, the other contender's eyes blink as he lunges in to strike. Tommy spins and delivers a powerful kick that knocks the attacker to the floor. The fellow's Sensi yells a warning, "Curtis, watch your guard!" The PA system carries across the auditorium, "3 points. Gold." 1 MINUTE WARNING BELL. Pressure shows on both fighter's faces. The black dragon opponent reaches to put Tommy into a chokehold - Tommy grabs and locks his opponent's arms - leans forward and flips the contender to the mat. THUD! Morgan Jeffrey and the entire Gold Eagle team shout out cheers! AUDITORIUM BUZZER. The Referee walks to the centre of the mat and Tommy and his opponent stand in flank position. They watch with anticipation as the Judges compare notes and converse quietly. The auditorium waits in excited silence. An elderly man edges to the microphone and speaks out clearly, "Tournament Winner is - Gold!" Tommy and his opponent shake hands and exit in opposite directions. Tommy walks back to his area with a new found confidence. He looks - and Sensi Jeffrey, Sarah and all his teammates have big smiles. Tommy descends off the mat and everyone gathers around to congratulate his victory. Morgan Jeffrey remarks, "Congratulations Tommy! You were excellent!" Sarah leans in with a happy smile, "Yay Tommy! - You won!" Tommy looks at his Teacher, "Sensi, I did what you said. He blinked before each attack. I was ready!" The rest of the Gold Eagle team crowd around Tommy bombarding him with High-Fives and pats on the back. Some mess up his hair. Tommy thoroughly enjoys it - he's all smiles.

TOURNAMENT AWARD CEREMONY

As the family, friends and spectators watch, all the various Dojos with their Sensis and teams stand before the Judges in neatly arranged groups. The Competition Officials award the respective Dojos their Tournament Trophies and the crowded auditorium loudly cheer and applaud. Sarah and Tommy stand in front of the Officials. Two Judges approach, each holding a tall shiny Trophy. Tommy glances over at Sarah - she smiles and gives Tommy a happy wink. One Judge presents Sarah with her award, and the other Judge hands Tommy his Tournament Trophy - Tommy stares at the shiny details. They both turn and rejoin their Gold Eagle Dojo group. Sensi Jeffrey and the fellow teammates greet the duo with cheers and celebration. The auditorium spectators clap their support.

Back at Gold Eagle Martial Arts Dojo, all the students are assembled in neat rows. Sensi Jeffrey places Sarah's and Tommy's trophies high up on the wall of awards. Tommy watches in awe. Sensi Jeffrey turns to address the class, "Congratulations again to Sarah and Tommy! Our trophy collection continues to grow. Remember class, you too can have a trophy up there! - Now, let's get back to training." The students pair up and practice their routines. Tommy and Sarah work as partners. Tommy moves with skill and confidence. Sensi Jeffrey observes and nods with approval.

Carl and Kathy peer out the kitchen window - Tommy is in the backyard practicing his Martial Arts routines. The teenager executes the moves with noticeable skill and speed. Tommy unleashes a barrage of punches, kicks and leg sweeps. To Carl and Kathy's shock and surprise - Tommy even does a backflip to land in a fight position. Carl turns to Kathy and exclaims, "He's coming along real fine!" Kathy replies, "Whenever I see him - he's always practicing, every chance he gets." Carl closes the kitchen curtain and looks at Kathy with gleeful expectation, "Any more of that pumpkin pie?" Kathy gives Carl a playful shove and quips, "I'll see what I can find." Carl smiles wide.

CHAPTER EIGHTEEN
Trouble At School

Ms. Mills hands out test scores to the class. Students' expressions range from frowns to broad grins. Ms. Mills stops beside Tommy's desk and hands him the paper face down and comments, "Keep up the good work Tommy!" Tommy turns over the paper and sees 82% at the top. He takes a deep breath - and stares at the mark. A big smile breaks across his face.

THE SCHOOL BUZZER

Students in class grab their books and backpacks and begin to exit the door. Outside the classroom, it's a high school traffic jam - the halls are clogged with throngs of kids moving to class. Tommy walks past some lockers and some brash townies block his path. He steps aside to go around, but two guys cut him off. Tommy finds himself corralled in the middle of the townies. One townie barks, "What's the big hurry - Rezskin?" Tommy scans the group and keeps his cool and replies, "Come on - I need to get to class!" The townies make fun of him with OOOO! And AWWWW! One guy knocks Tommy's books to the floor, and another townie kicks them away. Tommy eyes the culprits. The one kid challenges, "You have to go through us first!" Tommy replies, "I don't want any trouble - just want to get to class." One big guy leans in with a threat, "Guess what Rez - you got trouble!" By now, other students in both directions of the hall stop and watch the commotion. Some hold up their cell phone to video. The townies notice the crowd and get bolder. A townie speaks loudly, "You Rez kids are all the same - come to this school - but you don't belong! This is our school!" The group of townies start to push Tommy about. Tommy tries to stay upright. One townie throws a punch but the Martial Arts training kicks in and Tommy catches his fist and puts him in a wrist hold. The kid buckles to the floor. Another townie throws a punch - Tommy ducks and the fist strikes another townie in the face resulting in a bloody nose. At this point the kids jamming the hall begin to chant, "Fight! Fight! Fight!" Suddenly, there's an AIRHORN! Several teachers and the Vice Principal steer through the crowd of students. The teachers and Vice Principal exert their presence and authority. The Vice Principal looks at the townies and Tommy and orders, "I want to see all of you in my office - right now!" The other students quickly disperse to class and the hall soon empties. The teachers escort Tommy and the group of townies down the hall to the school office. Entering the office waiting area, the two male teachers point to the chairs and give the townies and Tommy that look - Sit Down! The townies sit on one side and Tommy finds a chair against the opposite wall. The townies try to stare down Tommy to intimidate him. Tommy simply keeps his cool. The Vice Principal calls in the students one by one. Tommy finally gets his turn to sit in front of the big desk. The Vice Principal looks at Tommy and asks, "How did this fight start?" Tommy gives him respectful eye contact, "I was just going to class - those guys jumped me!" The man with glasses, white short sleeve dress shirt and blue striped tie, opens Tommy's folder and looks through it. He peers over his eye glasses at Tommy and remarks, "It says here you were once arrested - in Court for a serious crime!" Tommy feels embarrassed by his past involvements and replies in a quiet voice, "Yes, that's true! - But that was before - in the past! I've changed!" The Vice Principal takes off his glasses and gives a stern look, "Well, fighting's not much of a change, son!" Knock! Knock! Knock! The Vice Principal remarks, "Come in." The School Secretary opens the door and steps inside holding a cell phone, and comments, "A student brought in their cell phone. You need to see this!" The lady hands the cell phone to the man and his eyes study the video taken during the hallway altercation. He pauses - hands the phone back to the Secretary and she exits and closes the door. The Vice Principal leans back and looks at Tommy sitting before him, and remarks, "It appears you didn't start the fight - just on your way to class." Tommy replies, "That's right Sir!" The Vice Principal closes the file and slides it to the side of the desk and remarks, "You can go now. This school incident has been sorted out. My apology for any misunderstanding!" Tommy stands to his feet, turns to exit the room, then pivots to address the administrator, "I know what I was like before - It's different now! I really want to learn!" The man smiles and responds, "Glad to hear that Tommy!" Tommy exits and closes the office door, walks past the Secretary and leaves the

School Office area - and steps out into the empty hall.

CHAPTER NINETEEN
The Practice Session

Carl steers the Chevy Malibu out of the driveway onto Plains Road, and drives through the Reservation past homes, stores and buildings until he reaches the Highway. He turns right and takes the Highway route for several miles then turns onto a Concession Road that leads to Canyon Run - Eli Water's horse ranch. Carl steers off the Concession onto the property's lane and drives toward the ranch house. As he gets closer he sees other vehicles parked near the long barn and large corral - Morgan's gold Dodge Mini Van, Barry's slate grey Chevy Silverado truck, and Steve's dark blue Ford F 150 pickup. Carl glances over and notices Eli's red Jeep Wrangler parked beside the house. He steers in and parks beside the other vehicles and exits his car. Carl walks over and slides open one of the large barn doors, enters inside and shuts the door. He scans the barn interior and spots his friends gathered in the wide sandy area in the structure's middle. Carl grins and starts to amble toward the group. As the guys stand in a casual huddle, Eli spots Carl approaching, smiles and calls out, "Glad you could join us today, brother!" Morgan, Barry and Steve turn around and wave a greeting to Carl, and he waves in return. As Carl joins them in the centre of the open arena, Barry asks, "How's Tommy doing?" Carl looks at the guys and replies, "He sure is coming along - trying his best at school (eyes Morgan) and doing really good in Martial Arts!" Morgan nods and remarks, "Tommy has caught on quick - he's a natural (grins) a bit like his grandpa! All the guys chuckle and Eli remarks, "Well guys, speaking of Martial Arts - we better get started with our monthly practice!" The men nod agreement and all begin to step back to form a large loose circle. Eli scans about and remarks, "Hand-to-Hand! Who's going first?" Barry replies, "Guess I will" and steps into the middle of the open space. Then, Steve steps into the middle opposite Barry, grins and remarks, "Brother, I hope you brought your 'A' game?" Barry laughs and quickly assumes a Martial Arts fighting stance and chides, "Bring it brother (chuckles) if you got it?" Steve grins as he shakes his head side to side - suddenly, Steve springs into a fighting stance and descends on Barry with a flurry of punches. Barry blocks Steve's series of punches, quickly pivots and counters with a roundhouse kick that Steve capably ducks. Steve jumps with a flying kick and Barry tilts his head to avoid impact. Steve lands in a fighting stance in the dirt behind Barry, who spins around to release swings and strikes and Steve deflects and blocks Barry's attack. Both men stop, move apart and step back. Steve grins and remarks, "I see you haven't lost your skills, brother!" Barry catches his breath and replies, "And you too brother - still quick and nimble." Steve and Barry exchange looks, bow respect and then rejoin the circle. Barry eyes his friends and asks, "Ok! Who's next?" Eli steps into the middle, looks around and remarks, "Sticky hands!" Carl walks into the middle opposite Eli. Both men raise and extend their arms out until the back of each man's hand is pressed against the other's. Eli grins with a friendly ribbing, "Hope you remember how to do this?" Carl smiles and replies, "Just try and keep up old friend!" Both men laugh as they begin to circle and rotate their hands together in unison. The purpose of 'Sticky Hands' is for both participants to keep their hands in continuous contact without breaking apart - the exercise is to test your opponent's skill and reflexes in Martial Arts hand-to-hand fighting technique. Steve, Morgan and Barry watch intently to see who will break first - Eli or Carl. The two friends lock eyes and concentrate as they move in synchronized harmony - their hands quickly turn, spin, rotate, push and pull in circular motions. Suddenly, Eli's hand slips and breaks away. The others yell, "Whoa!" Morgan cries out, "Carl's the winner!" Eli pats Carl's shoulder and grins, "Next time! I'll beat you next time, brother!" Carl smiles and the two step back into the circle. Eli remarks, "Morgan, you're the only one left." Morgan steps out and replies, "Time to perform the Dragon Kata!" The others smile and Barry pipes up, "I haven't seen that in a while." The Martial Arts instructor steps into the middle and quickly assumes a fighting stance - Morgan swiftly delivers a flurry of strikes at an imaginary attacker, spins with a roundhouse kick, then flip backwards three times into a fighting stance. He runs and summersaults to land on his feet to deliver fierce blows and punches to the front, left and right - then, Morgan moves into a Martial Arts stance and holds. Carl and the others clap their hands in approval, and Eli yells out in a teasing manner, "Great moves Morgan! Can I join your class?" Morgan rejoins the circle and remarks, "Only if I can learn how to shoot arrows like you!" Eli grins at Morgan's reply. Barry looks at everyone and comments, "And that brings us to weapons, right?" All the guys nod and make their way to the side of the barn interior that has tall wooden cabinet doors. As the guys approach the wall of cabinets and each stands before a compartment, Eli remarks, "Everyone's weapon has been cleaned and ready." Eli opens the door of the first cabinet and brings out a large black bow and black leather quiver full of black arrows. Steve opens the second cabinet and removes two dark long curved metal Indian war clubs. Barry opens the next cabinet and takes out a long black chain with a sharp black metal dart. Morgan opens his cabinet and removes his two black metal batons, each with an eagle claw on the end. The four hold their weapons and look at Carl as he opens the last cabinet and brings out the short black Ninjato sword and the long black Katana sword. He claps the swords and looks at his friends and comments, "Time to shine!" The five buddies walk back to the middle of the arena and reposition in much wider circle. Eli asks, "Who's going first?" Barry chimes, "I'll go" and he steps into the open area and holds the chain taunt with extended arms - he rapidly spins and twirls the chain to fire the dart in front, back, and side to side. Barry moves around as he quickly manipulates the chain dart with amazing skill and speed - then he stops. He looks at his friends and they all nod. As Barry gets back into the circle, Morgan steps into the centre and lifts his metal batons high in the air - then, Morgan crouches and swings the batons to the left and right, flips forward to rapidly swing the batons low to the ground and then up at head level. Morgan quickly pivots and delivers defence and offence moves to the front and back, then quickly spins into a fighting stance and holds. His friends clap as Morgan leaves the middle. Steve steps into the centre and positions his war clubs. He looks at his friends, then launches out with a series of blows, blocks and swings, as he swiftly moves in different patterns. The black war clubs twirl and rotate with precision. Steve displays great control and skill for attack and defence positions. Finished, Steve walks back to rejoin his friends as his buddies clap. Next, Carl steps into the centre and raises the Ninjato and Katana swords in a fighting stance. Carl quickly launches out with swift chops, slices and blocks, the two steel blades spin and twirl with blistering speed. Carl swings the Ninjato in front and the Katana in back at the same time, then, switches the Katana to the front and the Ninjato to the back. Carl spins and crouches low with sword slices at knee level, then spins to bolt upright with powerful sword swings at chest level. Then, Carl back-flips to land in a crouch with both swords in a battle position. He straightens up and looks at his four companions who smile and nod. The last one is Eli and all eyes are on him. Eli turns to face the back wall of the barn that has a row of targets. He removes two arrows from the quiver, fixes them on the bow and draws back the string and shoots. The two black arrows fly through air and each arrow hits a bullseye. Next, Eli takes out three arrows and positions them on the bow. Eli pulls back the drawstring and fires - three arrows zip through the air and each strike a bullseye. The others clap their approval! Eli glances at his buddies and remarks, "Watch this!" The men look at the back wall and see three tires suspended from the back rafters - each tire hangs by its own cord. Eli draws back the bow and shoots, the black arrow sails straight and cuts through all three cords to drop the tires. Thud! The four guys clap and cheer! Eli smiles and remarks, "Now that our monthly practice is over - I got a big table of food set up in the house - that's if you're hungry?" The guys break out with big smiles and Carl remarks, "Lead on brother - we're famished!" Each man returns his weapon to his cabinet, then they make their way out of the barn toward the house, chatting as they walk.

CHAPTER TWENTY

The Part Time Job

Carl and Tommy are seated at the dining table. Kathy sets out salad, bread and lasagna and sits down. The three pass the food around and fill their plates and begin to eat. Tommy looks at his grandpa and grandma and comments, "I'd like to get a part time job!" Carl and Kathy exchange glances and Carl remarks, "That's great Tommy! What kind of job you looking for?" The teen replies, Something that won't interfere with school or the Dojo. - Maybe some fast food places with flexible hours." Kathy gets up and goes into the kitchen and returns with an apple pie. She cuts and serves three portions. She glances at Tommy and mentions, "You should work weekends - that wouldn't affect your school or Martial Arts." Tommy digs into his apple pie ... and pauses, "You're right grandma! Lots of fast food places need part time help on weekends." Carl eyes Kathy and they both smile.

The next day, after school is over, Tommy stands at the town's road near the Highway that has all the fast food outlets. He takes a deep breath and starts to walk toward Flip Jack's Pancakes, opens the door to go inside and stands at the counter. He gets an attendant's attention to speak to the Manager. Tommy waits a few minutes, then a bald middle-aged man with shirt and tie approaches him. Tommy hands him a resume and asks about part time work. The man gives the resume a quick glance then shakes his head indicating - no! Tommy nods and thanks the Manager for his time and then he exits the store. Tommy lifts his eyes over to Primo Pizza. He walks on the sidewalk toward the store and goes inside. Tommy stands near the Host/ Hostess podium and asks to speak with the Manager then waits. Soon, a lady approaches wearing a dark jacket and white shirt and introduces herself as the Manager. Tommy hands her his resume and enquires if there are any part time openings? The lady shakes her head and replies no! Tommy smiles, says thanks and leaves the food outlet. Outside on the sidewalk, He notices the Chop Stick Express with its red neon sign. He decides to venture there and enquire. Tommy enters the business and looks around at the oriental decor and staff attire. He asks for the owner and an older man comes up to him. Tommy gives his resume and asks about any work openings. The man puts up his hand and motions no - then leaves. Tommy exits Chop Stick Express and ambles over to lean against a street light. At this point he's frustrated and getting discouraged. He stares at the ground for a bit then looks around and spots the brightly lit Burger Barn. He shrugs his shoulders and mumbles, "Why not!?" Tommy goes over and opens the store's front door and approaches the counter. There are three staff cleaning equipment and doing prep work. A teen behind the counter looks at Tommy and asks, "Can I help you?" Tommy replies, "Is the Store Manager here?" The staffer remarks to his coworker, "Go in the back and get Sam!" The coworker quickly disappears - and in a few minutes returns with the Manager. The man in his business shirt and tie gives Tommy a look over and asks, "Hello! I'm the Manager. What can I do for you?" Tommy smiles and hands the man his resume and asks, "Thank you for seeing me Sir! My name is Tommy Long Grass - I'd like to ask about part time work?" The Manager scans the resume and looks at Tommy and replies, "Let's go to the office and talk." Tommy comes through the counter and follows the Manager to his office at the back. The office is small and neatly organized. The Manager sits in his chair behind the desk and Tommy gets a chair in front and glances at the bulletin board arrayed with corporate memos, staff schedules and letters. The man takes a closer look at the resume and grabs a pen from a desk caddy and asks, "So Tommy, tell me something about yourself?" Tommy looks him straight in the eye and politely replies, "I live on the Reservation with my grandparents, and I'm a Sophomore at the District High School." The Manager comments as he jots some scribbles, "I don't see it on your resume. Have you ever worked fast food before?" Tommy is candid, "No Sir! I haven't (Smiles) But I'm a quick learner and a good worker!" The man leans back in his chair to relax and ponder, then glances at Tommy and asks, "Tommy, I like your attitude! (Eyes wall schedule) Can you come in this Friday night 6pm for training?" Tommy's eyes light up and with a wide smile he replies, "Yes Sir! I'll be here 6 pm sharp!" The Store Manager extends his arm and shakes Tommy's hand and remarks, "Welcome to the Burger Barn family! We'll see you Friday." Tommy responds with gladness as he shakes the boss's hand, "Thank you Sir! Thank you very much!" The man jots some notes on the resume, opens the file cabinet and picks out a folder and slides Tommy's resume in it. Tommy rises from his chair and exits the office and retraces his steps to the front. He goes through the service counter and walks out the front door.

Friday night at the Burger Barn…

The town's fast food strip is packed with all kinds of people buying food at the various outlets. Everyone is hungry and energetic, pumped with weekend excitement. In the Burger Barn, there's lots of orders and kids pack the interior waiting for their food. Tommy is decked out in his new Burger Barn employee outfit as he flips burgers and puts together hamburger orders behind the counter. The other experienced staff take the orders and handle the cash register. The Manager comes to the front counter area and checks Tommy's progress - he smiles and returns to the back office. In the parking lot next door to the Burger Barn, there's a custom car show featuring tricked out cars with glossy paint jobs, gleaming chrome, and eye-popping details. The owners proudly stand beside their rides as the weekend crowd mill about scoping out the vehicles on display. Next door people jam the Burger Barn to get eats. Tommy and the staff are super busy. The customer line-up is non-stop. Tommy assembles an order and takes it to the coworker at the cash register and sets it down on the counter. Tommy lifts his eyes - Spike is standing in front of him at the counter. Both momentarily freeze! Spike sneers and remarks, "Look who we have here!" Tommy replies, "Your order is ready." Spike gets tiffed and snipes, "What's wrong Homes forgot your old crew!" Tommy turns about and returns to the grill loaded with sizzling hamburgers. Other customers want their orders and they press in on Spike. The coworker checks the order receipt and tells Spike, "That will be $16.50 please." Spike hands the guy $20 and gets his change. He abruptly turns and jostles his way through the crowd and exits the front door. Standing outside - Spike is fuming mad and kicks a garbage can over scattering its contents. Spikes swags over to where his crew is hanging out near the car show. The rowdy crew greet Spike and quickly grab their food and start to chow down. Spike has a scowl and a gang member asks, "What's wrong man?" Spike gets angry and replies, "I saw Tommy! He works in there." The other crew members gather around as they munch their burgers. Another thug questions, "What you gonna do Homes?" Spike glances at his homies with a smirk and responds, "Only one thing to do - tell Bossman! Let him know! (heads for car) We gotta go!" The crew quickly jump into their rides and fire up the engines and peel out with squealing tires.

Somewhere out in the remote desert...

Spike and the crew pull their cars onto the grounds, and the armed lookouts let them pass into the sprawling auto yard. Spike and gang exit their rides and stride through the open large metal doors into the Northwest Gang hideout. The bright lit interior is filled with gangsters chopping vehicles and stacking auto parts. To the far right on an elevated platform is 'Command Central'. Bossman and key lieutenants with attractive babes, chill in a stylish tricked-out lounge, fitted with custom upholstered seats, crystal chandeliers, chrome and smoke glass coffee tables, overflowing liquor bar, and large screens for video games. Bossman sees Spike approach and stands to his feet. Spike feels nervous and stops a couple feet away. Bossman eyes the young thug who just disrupted his special time. Spike apologizes, "Sorry to interrupt you, Bossman!" The Top leader snarls, "What is it?" Spike takes a step closer, "Found out where that traitor kid works! - What do you want us to do about it?" Bossman stares at Spike and crew for a moment, then he gets a sinister grin and replies, "Wreck the place! Let 'em know that he's the reason! (Laughs) After that, no one will hire him!" Spike glances at his crew, then looks at Bossman and replies, "Done Boss! Just like you said!" Bossman turns around and gets back to relaxing and quickly has a babe attached on each arm. Spike and the crew hustle back through the warehouse interior and go directly to their cars, crank the engines and zoom off toward town.

CHAPTER TWENTY-ONE
Carl's Younger Days

Carl sits beside a small secluded lake nestled in the sandy terrain of the desert region. This is one of his favourite spots to visit and enjoy the peace and tranquility. The quiet of the untouched wilderness is broken only by the occasional call of a hawk and the sound of the desert wind blowing across the rugged surroundings. Carl drives out here sometimes so he can be alone to reflect and think things through - this time, his mind is on Tommy. Carl realizes his grandson is dealing with the changes brought into his young life; he knows because he sees the lad struggling with school, trying his best at the Martial Arts class, and avoiding any of the bad guys from his former gang. As his grandfather, Carl deeply cares for Tommy and wants the young lad to find a better life, and Carl's determined to do whatever it takes to make that possible. After all, the kid really has no one else; his older brother travels from one construction job to another never being home, and there's no other relative available to help. Carl picks up a small stone and tosses it into the water nearby - Plunk! He watches the ripples spread out across the water's smooth glassy surface, the stone makes circular waves that fan out and eventually disappear, the lake's surface returns to its mirror-like state. As Carl shifts his eyes across the lake's glassy appearance, his gaze stops at the water's edge and he looks at his reflection in the water. Thoughts of being a young lad like Tommy fill his mind as he remembers his younger days.

Carl is an eight year old kid, tall and lanky like a string bean. Other kids make fun of him because he's either too skinny or too tall, and some physically push him around. One day as young Carl sits alone pouting about how the kids make fun and pick on him, his grandfather Kamatsu, one of the old Shoshone warriors sits down beside him. Young Carl looks over, and his grandpa asks, "What's wrong - why are you sad?" Carl remarks, "I don't like feeling different and being picked on all the time!" Kamatsu leans in and gently whispers, "Do you want to learn to be strong - so no one can push you around?" Carl nods his head, then Kamatsu remarks, "You are old enough to begin training?" Carl asks with a puzzled look, "What training?" Grandfather Kamatsu places his hand on the lad's shoulder and replies, "Martial Arts! You will learn to be strong (Points) Strong in your body, your mind, and in your heart!" Carl's eyes brighten and he smiles and responds, "Yes grandfather! I'd like that kind of training!" The grandfather stands up and looks at Carl, "Tomorrow, I will begin to teach you (Kamatsu grins) Make sure you eat all your breakfast, tomorrow will be a long day!" As his grandpa leaves, young Carl smiles at the idea of getting strong enough not to be pushed around anymore!

The next day, bright and early, Carl stands with his grandfather in a wide open area with short grass situated a short distance in the woods. Kamatsu looks at Carl and comments, "You will train here in secret so others will not see. You will need to focus and work hard! - Can you do that?" Young Carl smiles and nods. The grandfather asks, "Stand like you do when you're with the other kids." Carl gets into his stand - and the grandfather reaches out and pushes the lad and Carl lands on the ground. The young lad gets up bewildered, and Kamatsu grins and remarks, "Let's begin with knowing how to stand so others cannot push you over." Carl likes that and smiles wide. Kamatsu instructs, "Copy how I position my feet and hold my body." As Kamatsu gives the example, Carl is keen to copy his grandfather's stance in every way. When the lad is fixed in position, Kamatsu reaches out and pushes from the back, the front, and the sides - the lad holds strong and solid. Carl is surprise and delighted! Carl remarks, "I didn't fall! I didn't fall! (Looks at grandpa) But why?" Kamatsu leans in with a smile and relies, "I showed you how to place your feet and body to stand strong and not be pushed over!" Carl chimes with eagerness, "Teach me more grandfather! I want to learn more." The old Shoshone warrior chuckles, "There are many more things for you to learn (waves his arm) as many things as there are different trees, birds, plants and animals!" Carl replies in excitement, "I'm ready grandfather! I want to learn it all!" Kamatsu nods at his grandson and comments, "Standing is just the start - in days ahead, I will teach you how - push back, block a punch, throw a punch, hold someone, and also break someone's hold. That is just the beginning!" Young Carl exclaims, "Teach me everything grandfather! I never want to be pushed around again!"

Kamatsu looks into the lad's young eyes and replies, "This kind of training is very special to make you strong to help yourself and to help others. Never use it to do wrong. Do you understand?" Carl stares directly at his grandfather and replies with confidence, "Yes grandfather - I understand!" Kamatsu smiles and nods, "Good little one! Very good! - I believe you will be a fine student!" Over the coming days, months and years, as Carl grows into a strapping teenager and a muscular young man. The Ninjan Master, Kamatsu, teaches Carl to use weapons like the Sickle, throwing Stars, the Tomahawk and the War Club. However, the weapon that Carl displays tremendous skill and ability with is the sword. The young man handles the Ninjato and Katana sword with great ability as he chops, spins, twirls, and slices the steel blades with precision and prowess. Eventually, Carl and Kamatsu spar with steel swords - the Ninjan Master executes swift slices, rapid chops, and quick thrusts - and Carl blocks, deflects, and counter attacks. When they both stop, Kamatsu smiles at his grandson's progress and proven skill.

A hawk soaring above calls out over the dry rocky landscape, and Carl emerges from his inner reflection. He stands to his feet and leaves the smooth flat rock where he sat, and walks to the Malibu parked a distance away. Carl stops beside the car and looks up as the hawk circles overhead. He smiles and gets into the Malibu, starts the engine and drives toward home.

CHAPTER TWENTY-TWO
Trouble Follows Tommy

The weekend crowd is lined up to order and the Burger Barn is packed with kids. Spike and the crew enter the premises and muscle their way inside - the street thugs shove, push and menace others out of the way. A couple boyfriends try to protect their dates, but the crew punch them out giving the boyfriends bloody noses and busted lips. Customers start to flee and exit the store. Now, Spike and crew have the entire store to themselves. The Manager and bewildered staff watch as Spike and his crew break windows, cut the seats, table tops, and walls with knives, smash light fixtures, and pour condiments all over the floor. The interior of the Burger Barn is a disaster - one huge mess! The Manager shocked and angry calls out, "Why are you doing this?" Spike swags up to the counter and looks the man in the eye and coldly replies, "Because of that Tommy kid you hired! He use to be one of us - we'll just keep on following him around (sweeps arm) and do more like this!" Spike and the crew scram out of the store and jump into their cars and peel away. The Manager runs out the windowless front door and catches a licence plate - and quickly scribbles it down on a piece of paper from his pocket. The man turns and goes back inside the destroyed interior, the workers are stunned and afraid. A couple girls are crying and the Manager and others try to console them. The Manager glances around the store's interior and surveys the damage.

POLICE SIRENS AND FLASHING LIGHTS.

The Police cruisers pull up and Officers quickly exit the cars and come into the store. An Officer remarks, "What happened here?" The manager approaches the Policemen and hands the piece pf paper and replies, "Some Street Gang came in here and started to trash the place. Fortunately, no one was hurt. (Looks at store) But this place is ruined!" A Policeman looks at the licence number and remarks, "Good work!

We can run this plate in our system." The Manager calls over his employees and releases them to leave the mess and go home. As the kids exit across the floor, they try to avoid the broken glass, smashed furniture, fixtures, and small pools of condiments. Outside the Burger Barn, Police stretch out the yellow Police tape to seal off the store - now a crime scene. A few minutes later, Tommy drives his Mustang toward the Burger Barn and sees the Police cruisers with flashing lights. He cautiously steers into the parking lot and stops. Tommy is surprised! He glances at the entrance - the front door just an aluminum frame with no glass, the stores windows are broken and have sections where sharp jagged glass protrude. Tommy sits in his car and stares at the wreckage. The Store Manager comes over and Tommy asks through his open window, "Sam, what happened?" The Manager replies, "Some gang came in - wrecked everything!" Tommy looks at his boss with concern, "Anyone get hurt?" The man replies, "No! Thankfully no one got injured - But the staff got really shook up - I sent them home!" Tommy gazes up at his employer and comments, "The store - it's terrible!" The man gazes down at Tommy and takes and deep breath and remarks, "That's why I have to talk with you!" Tommy looks up puzzled, "About what?" The man bends down eye level and replies, "Tommy, I like you! - You're a good kid and a good worker - But (Pause) that gang mentioned you by name and said they'd follow you around! I can't have that kind of trouble! I'm sorry Tommy, but I have to let you go!" Tommy is stunned and acknowledges, "I understand Sir!" At that moment, a big pickup truck advertising GENERAL CONTRACTING pulls up in front of the store and a large man gets out, and the Manager leaves Tommy and goes over to talk with the contractor. Tommy glances at the ruined business outlet, starts his car and pulls out of the parking lot and drives down the street.

Carl relaxes in his armchair as he reads the newspaper, and Kathy sits on the sofa and knits her afghan throw. They hear the Mustang drive onto the property and the engine cut out. A minute later Tommy comes in through the front door and goes directly to his room and slams the door. Carl and Kathy exchange concerned expressions. A few minutes later after he's cooled down, Tommy comes out of his room and sits on the sofa with a downcast expression. Kathy reaches out her hand to touch Tommy's shoulder and asks, "What wrong Tommy?" The teen looks at his grandparents and replies, "The Burger Barn let me go! No more part time job!" Carl puts down the paper and blurts, "What!?" Tommy turns to his grandpa, "The gang I ran with trashed the place - said they'll follow me around. The Manager got scared!" Kathy moves aside her knitting and scoots beside Tommy to console, "That's awful dear! - Don't let it get you down Tommy. We know you're trying - something else will turn up!" Tommy glances at his grandma with eyes full of worry, "If I get another job - the gang will just show up and make trouble! (Looks at grandparents) I don't know what to do?!" Tommy gets up and retreats to his room in brooding silence. Carl and Kathy sit quietly in deep concern.

CHAPTER TWENTY-THREE
Police Survelliance

The Police Precinct is busy! Officers at desks are working on files, and others are coming and and going as duty shifts change. An Officer at a computer screen uses the Police system to search the car licence number supplied by the Manager of the Burger Barn. He keys in the plate number and the system displays a photo ID, address, vehicle registration, and a criminal record. The Officer clicks the Print button and goes to the printer to retrieve copies. He takes the printouts to Chief Rogers's office. The Police Chief scans the information - looks at the subordinate and orders, "Get this information out to all our units - be on the lookout for this car!" The Officer nods affirmative and takes the info to the dispatch desk. A Police cruiser on patrol spots Spike's car and runs the plates - Confirmation! The two Officers tail Spike's vehicle from a distance and watch it pull into a residential property and four thugs exit the car and go inside the house. The Officer driving the squad car gets on the Police radio, "Unit 5 reporting. We followed the gang car to an address - 1816 Montgomery Drive. The suspects went inside the house. Over!" The Police Dispatcher responds, "The Chief will send an unmarked car for surveillance. Over-Out!" The Officer on the scene replies, "Ten Four!" The Police cruiser quietly pulls away from its location.

Soon, an unmarked car with two plain clothes Policemen pulls into a spot for the stakeout. Time lapses as the Officers watch and wait, and wait, and wait. Finally, the two undercover Officers see four gangsters leave the house and get into the vehicle, start the car and drive out onto the street and pull away. The unmarked cruiser starts up and follows. The gangster car travels through town streets unaware of the Police tail. The thugs drive onto the Highway and head toward the desert region. The undercover cops keep their distance. The suspect's car turns onto Pine Bluffs Road, the road sign is weathered and faded and barely readable. The stakeout team turn and follow with stealth keeping well back. After some considerable miles, out in the middle of nowhere, the gangsters pull into a large derelict property that's surrounded by a high galvanized fence and barbed wire. This was a thriving industrial auto yard that's no longer in business and sits abandoned and empty - or so it seems. The undercover unit stop their car in a hidden spot and watch through binoculars. Armed thugs appear and open the tall metal gate and let the suspect's car pass through, then they close the gate secure. An Officer in the stakeout vehicle picks up the Police radio, "Stakeout unit reporting in. The car entered an old abandoned auto yard located on Pine Bluffs Road. Armed gangsters are inside. Over!" The Police Dispatcher replies, "Come back to the Station. Chief Rogers wants a Precinct Briefing!" The Officer responds, "On our way! Ten Four!" The undercover Police car turns around and heads back to town.

CHAPTER TWENTY-FOUR

The Making of Bossman

Bossman stands on the raised lounge platform and surveys the sprawling gang hideout. He watches groups of men chop and dismantle numerous cars - sparks from welding torches and metal grinders spray the air, expensive engines are suspended on hoists, industrial racks are full of auto parts. Bossman glances to an array of shiny new vehicles parked nearby waiting for attention. The big man stares off into space...

FLASHBACK!

Bossman is a young skinny kid just surviving on the rough streets of an inner city project. Many buildings are rundown and in decay and sit abandoned with broken windows and gutted interiors. Young Bossman, whom the local thugs call "Lil' Bones" because he's so young and thin, acts as a 'lookout' for local pushers dealing drugs and other illegals. The kid sleeps in an abandoned building with some other street kids. To help get by, the kid goes uptown to shoplift stores and pick pockets in crowded city buses. Anything he steals and brings back, he barters with the local hoods for cash - but because he's young and naive, they rip him off many times. Still, to a street kid, a little of something is better than plenty of nothing! As Lil' Bones gets bigger and older as a teenager, he joins a neighbourhood street gang. Now, Bossman gets involved with drugs, violence and turf wars, and has run-ins with the cops. In one battle with another gang - the teenager kills a rival. The Police get a tip and Police cars descend upon the empty city lot where the fight takes place. Gang members see the cops and try to split - every man for himself. In the pandemonium, with gangsters and Police running in all directions - Bossman gets apprehended and arrested. Soon, he's before a Judge and sent off for incarceration. As a skinny teenager in Prison, Bossman gets beat up a few times - but each time he gets smarter, tougher, becomes a survivor. The young inmate starts to lift weights and eats everything the Prison Cafeteria can dish out. With little else to do behind bars, Bossman lifts weights and learns Martial Arts and practices 24/7. Over time, he becomes bigger, stronger and more lethal. In one Prison fight, Bossman breaks both arms of an attacker, and soon, Bossman's rep in Prison grows and he becomes respected and feared by the others. When Bossman is released from Prison, he starts his own street gang. His gang quickly grows in numbers and controls whole neighbourhoods. On the streets, as it was in Prison, Bossman is known and feared as a big mean brute with the muscle, street smarts and Martial Arts, to eliminate his foes. One day, the gang leader looks at the USA map and envisions expansion. Bossman begins to move his gang into other cities and eventually dominates entire regions. At this time, Bossman names his gang the Northwest Gang, and loyal gang members get NWG tattoos. This was when Bossman and the Northwest Gang invade the area towns and the Indian Reservation! Bossman claims the entire area as NWG Turf!

FLASHBACK ENDS

A gang lieutenant approaches the lounge platform and remarks, "Cars for Europe are ready!" Bossman barks an order, "Ship 'em off - we're a day late!" The lieutenant nods, turns starts to walk away, then turns to Bossman and comments, "I miss the big city! This place has nothing - just two-bit towns!" Bossman 'schools' his lieutenant and replies, "Nothing is why we're here, Homes! Less heat than LA! These cops are not the LAPD - we're cool!" The veteran thug nods with a grin and heads onto the chop floor and over to a bunch gangsters standing by expensive cars. Bossman gets out his cell phone and pulls up Contacts - Spike, then Bossman sends off a text - "DUMPSTER KID" - and presses Send. He leans against the lounge's chrome railing and waits a bit, and his cell BUZZES. Bossman checks Spike's reply text - "KID 2 DIE!" The big man smirks and pockets the phone.

Somewhere in town, Spike puts away his cell phone. He and the crew sit in their three tricked out cars in a parking lot. Spike looks at the guy in the front bucket seat and remarks, "Let's roll! Boss wants us to dumpster that traitor!" Spike sticks his arm out the car window to wave and signal the other gang members to move out. The three gang cars exit the parking lot and turn onto the road and start to cruise streets looking for their former associate. Spike and crew drive slow trying to find Tommy. Going past a number of streets, Spike turns a corner and spots Tommy's Mustang parked on the street. Up ahead, he sees Tommy and Sarah walking together on the sidewalk, and then they turn to enter a Gift Shop. Spike and the other two cars go further up the street to find some empty spots, they park beside the curb and cut the engines. Spike and his crew exit the cars and begin to walk back toward the store.

Inside the Gift Shop, Tommy and Sarah stand in front of a display of beautiful high quality porcelain figurines. A sales lady approaches with a friendly smile and asks, "Looking for something special today? (Eyes Sarah) Perhaps something for the young lady?" Tommy looks at the lady and replies, "Oh no! Sarah and I - we're just good friends - only good friends!" The sales woman looks at Sarah and smiles and remarks, "My apology! I just thought you were boyfriend and girlfriend. You both look so good together!" Sarah blushes. Tommy points to the figurines on the display shelves in front of him and comments, "I want to get my grandma a nice gift! She likes these kinds of things." The store clerk picks up a pretty figurine that's close and remarks, "These are exquisite! People collect them - and we're the only store in town that carry this product line." Tommy turns to Sarah and asks, "What do you think of these?" Sarah picks one up to examine and responds, "Very pretty! - your grandma will love it!" Tommy lifts his hand to move a stand of hair off his face, scans the display shelves, then points to a pretty figurine with brunette hair in a red dress and remarks, "That one! - Grandma looked like that when she was younger!" The sales lady retrieves the figurine and comments, "That's a beautiful choice! I'll wrap it up nice for you." Tommy, Sarah and the sales lady walk over to the store's sales counter. The clerk steps behind the counter, checks the price tag, then sets the figurine on the counter. The lady bends down and brings out a gift box with white wrapping tissue inside. The sales lady carefully lays the figurine in the soft layers of paper, covers it snugly with wrapping tissue, then tapes the box secure. Next, she unrolls and cuts some gold ribbon and ties the box with a fancy bow. Tommy raises his eyes brows and asks, "How much is it?" The lady holds the box and replies with a smile, "That will be $50 dollars please!" Tommy digs into his jean pockets and pulls out some crumples bills - and sorts out three $10 bills and one $20 bill. He hands the cash to the lady and the store clerk passes over the gift. Tommy turns to Sarah and mentions, "We gotta hurry back before grandma gets home! She's out getting groceries. As the two leave, Tommy tosses the gift box up and down in his hand. The sales lady is alarmed and quickly calls out, "Please be careful! - That's fine china!"

Tommy and Sarah emerge from the store, Tommy has the gift box under his arm. Suddenly, Tommy and Sarah are confronted by Spike and his crew of thugs. Tommy and Sarah step off the store steps to stand on the sidewalk. Spike swags up and gets in Tommy's face and snarls, "You shouldn't have ditched us, Tommy! Now we got orders to tidy up business!" Sarah steps in between Tommy and Spike and remarks, "We're not bothering you - leave us alone!" Spike looks at his crew and they all laugh! Spike turns to Tommy as he eyes Sarah, "We don't need little girls to interfere with big boy stuff!" The gangster grabs Sarah by her shoulder and shoves her aside. Tommy gets a serious expression, shakes his head side to side and remarks, "You shouldn't have grabbed her!" Spike replies with a smirk, "And why not?!" Spike no sooner has his words out when Sarah grabs and twists Spike's arm and powerfully kicks him into a parked car nearby. Before the crew can realize - Sarah spins around with a roundhouse that flattens a thug beside her. Now, the thugs on each side pull out knives, chains and pipes. Tommy and Sarah exchange a quick glance and Sarah remarks, "Just like we practiced last week!" Tommy nods his head. Tommy and Sarah quickly stand back to back. The gangsters attack from both sides. One swipes his blade and Tommy knocks the knife out of the attacker's hand, then Tommy delivers a Dragon Fist that flattens the guy. A big thug swings his steel pipe to hit Sarah - she kicks him hard in the 'family jewels' and he collapses on the sidewalk withering in pain. Two holding knives attack at the same time - Sarah blocks and counter-attacks. She grabs one's guy's arm to dislocate his shoulder, then rakes her nails across the other thug's eyes - causing momentary blindness. Other gangsters swing a chain and pipe at Tommy. He jumps aside to dodge the chain, grabs the guy's arm to flip him onto the cement. Tommy knocks the pipe out of the thug's hand and kicks him in the groin - he buckles in agony. The two thugs still standing look at their fallen comrades and put up their arms not to fight! POLICE SIRENS! Police cruisers zoom in and screech to a stop in the street. Officers quickly jump out to grab and arrest Spike and his crew. Officer Stibbs comes over to Tommy and Sarah and remarks, "What happened Tommy?" The trio watch as the Policemen take Spike and thugs into custody. Tommy looks at his Police friend and replies, "They jumped us! We just came out of the Gift Shop." Stibbs turns his gaze to the store and the lady clerk standing in the window and comments, "The sales lady called the Police - good thing she did!"

Spike and two other gangsters sit handcuffed in the back of a cruiser. The Police put the remaining thugs into the other squad cars. Tommy looks at the scene and remarks, "That use to be me once - No more Now!" Stibbs steps close and pats the teen's back and encourages, "You'e on the right path, Tommy! - Better days are ahead!" Tommy glances around and picks up the gift box and brushes off some street dust. He looks at Sarah and Stibbs and remarks, "My grandma's gonna love this gift! It's pretty like she is. (To Stibbs) We gotta get going!" Officer Stibbs watches as Tommy and Sarah walk to the Mustang, get in, and drive off down the street.

CHAPTER TWENTY-FIVE

Operation Desert Hawk

Police Chief Rogers holds a station wide Precinct Briefing, all Officers are in attendance. The meeting room is packed and everyone is buzzing about the reason for the important gathering. Chief Rogers stands at the front of the room and a senior Officer hands out information sheets to the assembled troops. When everyone gets the papers, the Chief speaks up, "Everyone pay attention! The Northwest Gang hideout is the old abandoned auto yard and warehouse out on Pine Bluffs Road. A Police raid named: Operation Desert Hawk, will be coordinated with SWAT and other Police jurisdictions. Okay everybody (Determined look) - Let's go arrest these gangbangers!" The Officers disband and exit to their cruisers. Cars trunks open up and the Police put on their bulletproof vests and get tactical weapons - semi-automatic submachine carbines, combat shotguns, riot guns, and ballistic shields. The Officers get fitted and stand battle ready. Police Chief Rogers exits the Station and goes to his cruiser and pops the trunk. He grabs his ballistic vest and straps it on, then reaches in and gets the 16mm assault rifle. The Police Officers assemble around the Chief and wait instructions. Chief Rogers looks at his men and remarks, "Listen up! SWAT, State Troopers, and Tyler Units are working with us. We drive to Miller Junction - there's a big gravel pit there - that's the rendezvous point!" The Policemen nod acknowledgement and Chief Rogers and the Officers get into their Police cars and pull out of the parking lot. People in town watch with curiosity and interest as the line of cruisers go through the town streets and head toward the highway.

Later on, Police Chief Rogers and the Officers drive into the large gravel pit. The steep sides provide excellent concealment for the rendezvous. Before them in the wide open area normally used for the big dozers and shovels, are State Trooper squad cars, the SWAT armoured vehicle, and Tyler Police cruisers. Armed Troopers and Officers and the SWAT team, are gathered in groups. Chief Rogers and his force drive up, park and get out of their cars and walk up to the other units. Chief Rogers approaches the SWAT Commander, then waves over the Trooper and Tyler leaders, When all four are together, the SWAT Commander pulls out an area map and they study it as the Commander remarks, "The access points are here and over there. We know from intel that they have heavy firepower at the gates - likely inside the warehouse too!" Chief Rogers injects, "We have the element of surprise!" The SWAT Commander faces Chief Rogers and remarks, "This is your jurisdiction - so you have the lead in this Operation! What do you want us to do?" Chief Rogers looks at the map and the outline of the gang headquarters and replies, "Attack from two access point simultaneously! Take out their guards. SWAT at the front door - Troopers at the back door! Once inside the property we storm the warehouse!" The State Trooper Captain remarks, "Sounds like a right good plan!" The Tyler Captain exclaims, "Been waiting to get this gang! - They totally ruined our town!" Police Chief Rogers looks at the three leaders, "Let's do it then! - Take 'em down!" The four Police leaders disperse, each one going to their own men. All the Officers double check their pistols, assault rifles, shotguns, and grenade launchers - all locked and loaded! Operation Desert Hawk is in full force, and the Police Units get into their vehicles and head out of the gravel pit.

CHAPTER TWENTY-SIX

Bossman Orders A Wicked Deed!

An area grocery store is busy with people getting groceries. The parking lot is full of vehicles coming and going. Kathy drives in and finds a spot midway in a row and parks her car. She exits and grabs a shopping cart and enters the store's sliding entrance doors to disappear from view. Tucked away, a few rows over, is the black sedan with dark tinted windows. Inside the car, a gangster is on his cell phone, "Bossman - she's here! - just went inside." The thug's phone speaker carries Bossman's reply, "you know what to do!" The gang lieutenant hesitates a bit then replies, "In broad daylight? With witnesses?" Bossman barks, "Just follow my orders!" The gangster replies, "Done Boss! Just like you want!", then he ends the call and pockets the phone. The Northwest Gang lieutenant and three big thugs sit in the sedan and wait…and wait. After a while, Kathy comes out of the store pushing the shopping cart loaded with groceries. She wheels the grocery cart near the back of her car, pops the trunk and begins to load in the bags of grocery. As Kathy leans in to place a bag, suddenly, the black sedan screeches to a stop and two big thugs quickly exit and grab Kathy! The woman screams and struggles trying to break free. One thug flings open the sedan's back door and the two brutes physically throw Kathy into the back seat and slam the door shut! The black sedan roars away. Meanwhile, customers had heard Kathy's screams and witnessed the abduction - one lady is on her cell phone calling 911.

The black sedan tears across remote desert roads and Kathy sits in the back seat between the two thugs. She glances at her abductors and quickly reaches to grab the handle to open the door. The thug stops her and she fights with him; in the tussle, top buttons on her blouse get ripped. The guy grabs her arm to hold her and she bites his hand - he yells and smacks his palm her across the face - Kathy's nose bleeds. She desperately pleads, "Let me go! Please! I won't say a thing to the Police - just let me go!" The gangsters are silent and stone-faced. After a brief lull, Kathy tries again to escape from the car and the thugs rough her up; now, Kathy sits captive with messy hair, torn blouse, bruises and a bloodied nose. She stares out at the desert as the car speeds toward the gang hideout.

The black sedan drives onto the property and slams on the brakes spraying stones and dust. The lieutenant and gangsters exit and standby. A big thug yanks Kathy out of the car manhandling her. She fights back and her blouse sleeve gets torn. The gangsters march Kathy into the cavernous warehouse, across the busy shop floor, and through a steel door into a dingy dim lit room with a rusted overhanging florescent light. Kathy struggles but to no avail. One thug forces her to sit in the tarnished metal chair while another thug ties her feet and arms secure to the heavy object. Kathy's face shows courage and defiance! She eyes her captors with distain. Tied to the cold steel chair, Kathy sits alone - vulnerable - exposed. Her blouse is ripped and the missing top buttons reveal her smooth skin and traces of her womanly form. All across the shop floor, curious gangsters stop work and walk toward the side room where they saw the woman was taken. The room starts to fill with rough looking men covered with sweat, grease and grime - each one jostling to get a better look at the attractive woman tied to the chair. The onlookers leer at her. Kathy looks into their eyes and finds no pity - no mercy - no help - just wanton desire! A loud voice bellows from the back of the crowd, Bossman barks, "Back off! I said back off!" The men quickly disperse to clear a path for Bossman. He saunters up and stands in front of Kathy and she lowers her eyes to the floor. Bossman steps closer and towers over her and remarks, "Hope you find the accommodations to your liking? Best I could do on short notice!" Kathy lifts her gaze and looks directly into the brute's eyes, "You did wrong coming onto our lands! These are Indian lands - Sacred!" Bossman squats down eye-level and replies in a pompous tone, "These are my lands! Northwest Gang lands! (Thugs cheer) This territory belongs to us now! (Looks at her) You belong to us now!" The men yell and cheer more! Kathy stares back and replies adamantly, "I belong to my husband! - and no one else!" Bossman brushes his rough hand down her cascading hair, his hand slides along the front of her torn blouse - and stops near her visible cleavage. Kathy grimaces and turns her face away. Bossman places his hand on Kathy's head and forcibly turns her face toward him and coldly remarks, "You belong to your husband! - That's exactly what I'm counting on pretty lady!" Kathy in anger spits on the hoodlum's face and yells, "You're nothing but sticking trash! - Pure filth!" Bossman stands up, wipes the spit off his cheek and tilts his head to crack his neck. He calls over a lieutenant and whispers in the man's ear and the underling looks at Kathy and nods. Bossman turns around and looks at the group of men and callously announces, "Boys! - She's all yours! Show her a good time!" The men part and Bossman walks out of the room laughing. The men begin to close in around the frightened lady as Bossman leaves the office - Kathy screams repeatedly!

Carl is in the living room when his cell phone BUZZES. He greets the caller, "Hello!" Bossman's voice replies, "I have your wife! - She's a fine looking woman!" Carl is shocked and alarmed and quickly replies, "Whatever you want, deal with me! Leave my wife out of it!" Bossman stands outside the former warehouse office and holds his cell phone in the air - Kathy is crying and screaming! The thug asks, "Do you recognize that voice? - The voice of your wife?" Carl is livid and retorts, "What do you want?" Bossman laughs and replies with a sinister chuckle, "What I want! What I want is for you and me to fight! Fight me! - If you win, you get your wife back!" Carl paces to and fro across the living room with the phone to his ear. He shutters at Kathy's cries and sobs in the background. Hearing his wife's distress, Carl boldly declares, "I'll fight you! Fight you man-to-man! (Pause) The old steel factory near Snake River!" Bossman revels at the reply he's waiting for and remarks, "Like I said - you beat me, you get your wife back - If not, well too bad! - Old man, get ready for the beating of your life!" The call ends.

At the warehouse, Bossman pockets his phone and circles his arm high in the air - the Boss's signal to move out. Thugs see the leader's sign and gangsters across the warehouse rally and run toward their vehicles parked in the big auto yard. Armed thugs jump into cars, SUVs, pickup trucks and cargo vans. The gangsters carry automatic rifles, semi-automatic pistols, machetes, chains, clubs and knives. Bossman strides over to a big black SUV with black tint windows, opens the driver door and climbs up to the rocker panel for all to see. Bossman raises his arm and flags it forward - then gets inside, fires up the engine and peels out. Vehicles across the auto yard ignite their engines and tear out. From a bird's eye view, it's a long convoy of gang vehicles following Bossman's big black SUV.

CHAPTER TWENTY-SEVEN
The Ninjans Get Ready

Carl goes into the master bedroom - pushes on a false wall that opens to expose a jet black wooden cabinet. He dials Morgan's number and his friend answers, "Hello Carl!" Carl remarks in a serious tone, "That big city gang has Kathy! Their leader wants to fight me. If I win - Kathy goes free! (Pause) Call the others! We meet at the old steel mill." Morgan responds, "We'll be there!" Carl pockets his cell phone and swings open the cabinet's black doors to reveal an arsenal of weapons - swords, sickle, tomahawk, bow and arrows, knives, chain dart, blow pipe, metal stars, bombs, poisons, climbing rope and metal claw. A black Ninjan outfit hangs in the back. Carl quickly dons his Ninjan clothing and affixes weaponry - the long Katana sword and the shorter Ninjato sword, tomahawk, knives, stars, bombs, and rope. His dark form now bristles with instruments of death. Carl grabs some short containers and twists off the lids. He faces a wall mirror, then dips his fingers into the containers to smear on War Paint to create a fearsome look! Carl returns the false wall that hides the black cabinet, then he dashes out of the bedroom, across the living room and out of house - leaving the front door wide open.

An hour later Tommy and Sarah drive onto the property and park the Mustang. As they exit the vehicle they notice the front door is wide open. The duo walk to the house, Tommy holds the gift box in his hand. He remarks to Sarah, "That's odd! Grandpa doesn't like the front door left open! (Scans about) And I don't see grandma's or grandpa's car!?" Sarah responds, "Where are they? - out back?" Tommy and Sarah reach the front stoop and ascend the steps and go inside and look around. Tommy calls out, "Hello grandpa! - Grandma? - Anyone here?" Silence. Tommy goes to stand in the middle of the room and Sarah follows. As Sarah stands by, Tommy looks in the kitchen, the hallway, the master bedroom, the backyard - Nothing! He enters the living room and plops down in a dining chair with a dejected expression. Sarah tries to comfort and suggests, "Call their cell phones. Maybe there was a quick errand to run!" Tommy pulls out his cell phone and dials his grandpa's number. Ring! Ring! Ring! No answer! Then he dials his grandma's number. Ring! Ring! Ring! Again, no answer! Tommy looks at Sarah with worry, "Called both - Nothing!" Tommy sits at the table puzzled and perplexed. Sarah sits down beside him to console, "Let's just stay here and wait for them. - they shouldn't be too long!" Tommy nods and gives Sarah a faint smile and replies, "You're right! Grandpa and grandma will be back soon!" The two teenagers sit pensive and quiet - with the front door still open, they can see and hear the vehicles going by on Plains Road.

CHAPTER TWENTY-EIGHT

Shoot Out At The Auto Yard

Police Chief Rogers, Officers, SWAT reach the gang hideout and get into position. The Troopers and the Tyler Unit are prepped in the back location. Police Chief Rogers speaks into his handheld Police radio, "All units - GO!" The armed thugs guarding the metal gate are relaxed and distracted. Suddenly - CRASH! The SWAT armoured vehicle smashes through the gates leaving only crumpled twisted sheets of metal behind. Police cars directly follow the SWAT vehicle into the auto yard grounds. The armed thugs are taken by surprise, many scurry into the warehouse and shut the big steel doors. The armed gangsters still outside fire their automatic rifles and pistols at the Police. Officers quickly exit cruisers to take cover behind car doors and vehicles and return fire. At the same instant - gunfire erupts from the back gates of the auto yard. Automatic rifle fire. Pistol rounds. Shotgun blasts. The Police target the thugs shooting the automatic rifles - it's an intense firefight! Hot lead flies everywhere, automatic guns spray bullets that puncture cruisers with lots of bullet holes, some Officers get hit and wounded. SWAT and the Police set their sights on the automatic fire and take out the bad guys. Chief Rogers and the Policeman emerge from cover and rush the warehouse. The distant gunfire stops - then silence. Almost immediately, State Troopers and Tyler Police come around the far end of the long warehouse. They join up with Chief Rogers and the others. The Trooper Commander reports, "The back is clear! But we saw gangsters go inside." Chief Rogers looks at the SWAT Commander, and remarks, "SWAT will ring the door bell!" The Commander grins and replies, "That's what we do best!" The Policemen get into position and watch as the Armoured car rams the sealed entrance doors. BANG! The steel doors buckle and break wide open. The SWAT armour car zooms into the warehouse interior and skids to stop a couple feet from some expensive sports cars. The Officers race inside and spread out for cover. The cavernous interior is brightly lit by overhead florescent lights - the Police scan the interior and see cars, SUVs, trucks, that are chopped and dismantled. Chief Rogers gets the Tyler Commander's attention and orders, "Go to the back exit - make sure no one escapes!" The Commander replies, "No one will get past us!" The Tyler Commander with pistol in hand, waves to his men to follow as he exits the open warehouse entrance. Gang members are concealed throughout the vast warehouse, hiding behind vehicles, steel pillars, industrial equipment and racks of auto parts. The thugs open fire and the Police shoot their guns. An intense firefight! Bullets ricochet and bounce off the cement floor, steel columns and metal parts. One macho thug lieutenant steps out from behind a steel pillar and unloads his assault rifle at Police positions. As the thug exchanges ammo clips - SWAT blast him dead! Leaderless and scared, a couple gangsters raise their hands to surrender. Police Chief Rogers yells out, "You're trapped - surrounded! Give yourselves up!" He listens for a response - silence, then there's sounds of movement and weapons being thrown on the cement floor. Slowly, individual gang members rise to surrender with their hands in the air. Soon, all the remaining gangsters are in the open with both arms high in the air. From various positions - Officers, Troopers and SWAT approach with their weapons trained on the criminals. The SWAT Commander orders, "Lay face down with open hands extended in front of you! Stay that way - Don't move!" The Police rush in to put the criminals' arms behind their back and cuff them. Once secured, the Officers help them to their feet. The gang members look defeated and whipped. Chief Rogers approaches and asks, "Where's your leader? (Walks between them) Where's Bossman?" The thugs eye each other and remain tight-lipped - no one talks! Then, a young man in his early twenties starts to open his mouth, "He went..." An older thug eyes him and threatens, "Say nothing! Don't give them anything!" Chief Rogers steps up and looks the young man eye-to-eye and speaks in a fatherly tone, "Never mind him, son! Tell me what I need to know." The young man replies, "Bossman took most of the gang to a big fight! - that's what I heard." Chief Rogers questions, "Where's this big fight?" The young thug replies, "Something about an old steel mill - somewhere in the desert." Police Chief Rogers looks at the young man, "Thank you son! I'll remember your help when I fill out my report (turns to Officers) Some of you spread out, see if any are hiding!" The Policemen fan out and search the large warehouse interior. An Officer enters the defunct warehouse Office, and to his shock, he discovers Kathy on the cement floor badly beaten with signs of abuse! He calls out, "Chief. There's a civilian - a lady hurt bad and needs medical attention!" Chief Rogers and two Commanders enter the room and see Kathy with noticeable signs of trauma. Chief Rogers immediately uses his radio mic, "Dispatch. Send a Paramedic ASAP! We have an injured civilian in need of urgent medical care!" The Dispatch staff replies, "Ten Four. Ambulance on the way!"

Moments later...

The ambulance with lights flashing zooms into the auto yard and Officers guide them to the warehouse entrance. The back doors of the ambulance open and the paramedics spring out carrying a Jump Bag and a Trauma-Spine Board. They race inside and the Police direct them to the office. The paramedics see Kathy unconscious and rush to the victim, Chief Rogers and the SWAT Commander step aside to make room. The paramedic with the Jump Bag quickly inspects Kathy's vital signs. His partner positions the Trauma Board beside her body. As one paramedic turns Kathy on her side, his partner slides the Trauma Board underneath her body, then they ease Kathy onto the board and strap her secure. With a paramedic on each end, the two ambulance workers lift Kathy and quickly take her to the ambulance. Inside the Ambulance, one paramedic starts an I.V. drip in Kathy's arm, then he fastens leads from electronic medical equipment to her body. Beep! Beep! - Beep! The other paramedic preps a hypodermic needle and injects Kathy with antibiotics. He watches the heart monitor. The other paramedic closes the ambulance back doors, and gets behind the wheel, starts the vehicle and pulls out with the sound of the siren and emergency lights flashing. Police Chief Rogers, the Commanders and the Policemen watch the ambulance leave the auto yard and race off. Chief Rogers looks at the arrested gangsters huddled together in a group awaiting transport. He watches as Officers put them into the back seat of cruisers, then the Offices drive off. Chief Rogers radios the Station and remarks, "Dispatch. Requesting more ambulances and a helicopter to go to the old steel factory near Snake River. Over!" Police Dispatch replies, "Ten Four! Ambulances and helicopter notified. Over!" The Police Chief urges, "Tell them to hurry! Ten Four! Out!" He waves the Unit Commanders over and the leaders gather around. The State Trooper Commander asks, "What's the next move!" Chief Rogers looks at the Commanders and replies, "We head for an abandoned

Steel Mill in the desert at Snake River. Bossman took his Gang there to fight - Who we don't know?" But no one will be expecting us. Let's roll!" All the Police get into their vehicles and wait. Chief Rogers gets into his cruiser and flips on the flashing Police lights and peels out of the Auto yard. SWAT and the other Police follow Chief Roger's cruiser. The column of Police cars with flashing red and blue lights fade and become smaller as the Police Units travel farther into the desert.

CHAPTER TWENTY-NINE
The Big Battle

The old derelict Steel Mill sits in the rugged terrain out in the middle of nowhere. Abandoned broken buildings, rusted industrial machinery, neglected storage tanks, and large scrap heaps of discarded metal. The facility and site stand in eerie silence to its once busy productive past. Carl drives onto the property and takes his car across the large gravel lot and steers around a tall metal tank to park hidden away. He exits his car and scans around. Carl looks out to see four figures dressed in black rise from secluded positions. Morgan and the other Ninjans wear fierce War Paint - each brandishing their weapon specialty. Morgan holds up the two metal batons, each club with an eagle claw on the end. Barry swings the black chain dart to produce a whirling sound as the chain twirls through the air. Steve stands with a curved War Club in each hand. Eli stands layered with quivers of black arrows and raises up his large black bow. Carl pulls out his two gleaming swords and lifts his arms high in the air. - The Ninjans are ready for battle! Carl and the Ninjans set up tripwires linked to explosive charges. The Ninjans separate and take up ambush points - and wait. Morgan makes a bird call to get Carl's attention and points - the Ninjans look at the cloud of dust that rises in the distance. Carl prompts his fellow Ninjans, "Get ready - They're almost here!" The Ninjans keep out of sight and focus on the upcoming battle!

Bossman peers through the windshield and sees the dilapidated Steel Mill off in the distance. He presses the pedal to accelerate and zooms toward the factory, the long convoy of gang vehicles race to keep up. Excited and eager for a fight, the convoy of gangsters brandish their weapons out the vehicle windows - wildly yelling and displaying their submachine guns, 9mm pistols, shotguns, machetes, crowbars and knives! Bossman and his Northwest Gang drive past the chain link perimeter fence and roar onto the large gravel lot. Bossman and his thugs jump out and mass together - their numbers and firepower reveal a small army! Gang members are hyped up and edgy - Bossman puts up his hand in the air and everyone freezes, no one moves. The big man looks across the weathered industrial setting and squints his eyes to focus - no one - nothing there! Bossman brings his cupped hand beside his mouth and yells loud, "Old man! - Indian! - You here?" Only silence except for the crickets. A lieutenant leans in and comments, "Boss, maybe we got here first?" Bossman turns and pushes the guy aside and steps out a few more paces and bellows, "I know you're here! Come out and fight! - Like we agreed." Bossman turns to his crew and smirks. The eerie silence makes the gangsters nervous. Individual thugs point their weapon around at shadows, fidgety hands grip machetes and knives. Suddenly, Carl stands atop a steel tank some distance away and calls out, "The fight is between you and me! - not your entire gang!" The big thug glances at his soldiers and replies, "Where I go - my crew follow. Too bad you're outnumbered (looks at automatic weapon) and outgunned!" Carl boldly replies, "You don't have any honour!" Bossman spits on the ground, smirks and answers with bravado, "I have a gang - I don't need honour!" Carl quickly retorts, "That's what I figured!" Bossman taps a thug on his left to fire his automatic weapon at Carl. The thug unloads and bullets strike all around - Carl ducks for cover. Whoosh! A black arrow plunges deep into the shooter's leg bucking him to the gravel. Gang members blast away at Carl's location and bullets ricochet off metal surfaces. Suddenly, Carl pops up in another location visible to all. The gangsters shoot their guns at him, but Carl disappears. Bossman looks around at his men and sees the empty casings on the ground and yells, "Stop! Hold your fire! Don't waste your bullets - he's playing us. Just an old Indian scared and hiding. Everybody fan out. Let's get him!" The gangsters disperse into small groups and move forward to look behind bins and machinery, around corners, in containers, and under conveyor belts. One big thug steps between two steel drums and breaks a tripwire - BOOM! The blast breaks loose large metal pipes and supports that fall on top the big thug and crew members with him. The four thugs are injured and put out of action. Another set of gangsters go in the direction of the explosion to investigate - and run into Morgan. The Ninjan flails the metal batons with devastating effect. The three gangsters lay on the ground bruised, beaten and unconscious. The gang's numbers have just declined - eight thugs out of commission! Bossman eyes the fallen comrades, then looks at his remaining force and smirks - he feels his crew is still large - he still has forty armed thugs that can move and fight!

Carl stands at the open entrance of the first factory building, a long industrial shed that houses heavy machinery and equipment to make steel. Carl taunts and teases the criminals, "You're so many - and still can't get me!" Bossman grits his teeth in anger and waves his arm and the gangsters rush forward toward Carl. He watches and gages their approach - then disappears inside. The Northwest Gang descends on the building and spill into the cavernous room. Their eyes need to adjust to the dark interior. Shafts of sunlight pierce the interior here and there to illuminate the factory floor and equipment. Bossman and the gangsters fan out - weapons ready! The thugs are cautious as they creep deeper into the dusty old facility, They stop to listen - move ahead - stop to listen - then move ahead! TWIRLING SOUND! One gang member turns about - a metal dart is imbedded in his leg calf. Suddenly, the dart is yanked out to disappear into the shadows. The dart zips out from the shadows and sinks into his other leg - the gangster crumples to the floor unable to move. Gang companions fire their guns in a barrage of hot lead - bullets ricochet everywhere. As the gangsters continue to creep forward - going between the equipment and large machinery - Steve attacks with his War Clubs. Thugs are pummelled and knocked out - their guns and machetes drop to the cement floor. Clang!

MULTIPLE EXPLOSIONS! FIREBALLS!

A gang lieutenant sees the flickering shadow of flames outside. He and a bunch of others run out of the building to investigate. They're all stunned! Bossman and the rest join them at the shed's entrance. The glow of flames dance across their faces - gang vehicles are ablaze. As fire reaches the gas tanks, other gang vehicles EXPLODE! Not a single gang vehicle is spared - every car, van, SUV and truck are on fire! Carl's loud voice echoes from inside the building, "None of your gang can leave! You and your gang made a terrible mistake coming into this territory!" Bossman and the gangsters in crazed anger blast their guns everywhere at the empty shadows. Halfway down the building, Carl stands on top heavy machinery illuminated by a shaft of sunlight - it looks like he's under some kind of spotlight. Bossman barks to his crew, "There he is! - Get him!" The NWG members give chase and Carl turns and runs toward the building's large back exit doors. Bossman and the gangsters are in hot pursuit!

Carl runs into the second industrial building just ahead of the gangsters. The thugs stop and gather at the second building's doorway - cautious and wary. Bossman directs his troops, "We will corner him! One group go to the back exit and flush him toward us." The NWG force divide in two, and one group runs around the long industrial shed to its back exit doors, and move in with their guns ready. The late afternoon sunlight lessens and more effort is needed to see inside the shadowy confines of the structure. As a gangster steps forward into a shaft of sunlight - WHOOSH! A black arrow sinks into his right thigh and he topples to the concrete floor in pain. A gang member bends down to assist the fallen homie, and a black arrow goes through the young man's shoulder - he bellows in agony! Bossman motions the gang to keep watch above where the arrows came from. The gang leader and henchmen carefully inch along into the shed's interior. Four thugs scour the area to the left side of the interior - each welds a machete. Suddenly, Morgan springs out and the thugs swing wildly at him, the sharp machete blades slice dangerously close to his face and torso. Morgan swiftly ducks and blocks the machete attacks, and strikes the assailants with powerful blows to disarm and render them useless. Two thugs lay on the floor unconscious, the others wither on the ground in a world of hurt! The sounds of fighting brings more gang members over - but Morgan quickly vanishes into the dark recesses of the factory equipment and large machines. Bossman and his gang converge and see their fallen comrades. A gang lieutenant voices his concern, "We lost 6 more! - Now we're only 34 strong." Bossman looks at his underling and remarks, "So what! - The old Indian has a couple friends. It doesn't matter - soon, they'll be dead men! (Eyes gang) Spread out - let's get 'em!" In the middle of the long shed, Carl and his fellow Ninjans gather behind a giant foundry bucket - Carl, Morgan, Steve, Barry and Eli meet to update and plan. Carl comments, "Keep drawing them in!" Morgan replies, "They're running out of bullets - and courage too!" Barry remarks, "Their leader is a tough hombre! For him - it's do or die!" Carl glances at his friends and replies, "Leave their boss to me - we have unfinished business!" The four Ninjans nod agreement and they all disperse in separate directions toward different areas of the shed. By this time, the second group of thugs have entered through the back doors. The thugs spread out and check spaces as they work their way toward the front. Bossman and his group meet them in the middle. The leader questions his men, "See anything?" The lieutenant replies, "No Boss! It's like they disappeared." Bossman scans the interior, then waves his hand forward, and the assembled thugs move ahead with great caution. The criminals point their guns, machetes, clubs and knives in every direction. Suddenly, Steve throws smoke bombs in their path. POOF! POOF! POOF! Thick clouds of grey smoke fill the air. Swiftly, the Ninjans attack the confused and disoriented enemy with speed and ferocity - a barrage of black metal stars sail through the air to strike arms, legs, hands and torso. Carl and fellow Ninjans deliver strikes, blows, kicks and punches to bring down assailants left and right - the factory floor strewn with incapacitated thugs, unable to move or fight. When the smoke clears the Ninjans are gone - Scared and angry, the gangsters curse and fill the air with vulgar outbursts as they blast their automatic rifles, shotguns and pistols in all directions. Bullets ricochet across the shed. Bossman looks around - gang numbers are down to half - now only 17 thugs are with him. A lieutenant remarks with concern, "Boss, we should cut out! Half our guys are down!" Bossman chides him, "Shut up! (Waves his pistol) Only takes one bullet to end a man's life! And we've got slugs for each one of them. - Come on!" Bossman and his remaining thugs creep through the latter portion of the shed - Nothing! The gangsters see the open exit doors that lead to the back lot with heaps of scrap metal and rusted heavy equipment. Bossman and his crew walk out the back doors toward the piles of twisted metal and jagged steel.

The scrap yard is a jumble of rusted machine parts, steel plates, jagged metal cuttings, steel filings, twisted rebar, and large coils of industrial wire. The gangsters insert fresh ammo clips and Bossman directs them to fire their guns at the piles of scrap. Bullets fly and ricochet. Bossman and the gang stop shooting and wait - Nothing! The gang spread out and scale the large metal heaps to try and flush Carl and the others out. The gangsters step across the piles of discarded metal - their movement and body weight makes loud noises - CREAKS! SCRAPING! CLANGS! BANGS! On the far left, a thug spots Steve and fires his assault rifle. As bullets spray across the steel parts - one bullet tears into Steve's right side and he topples to the ground. The gangster exclaims proudly, "I got one! He's down!" The gangsters rush over to the fallen Ninjan, and a thug kicks away Steve's war clubs. A big thug kicks Steve in the face! Another thug swags over and points his pistol at Steve's forehead. The Ninjan is weak and gasps for breath. Bossman strides over and looks down with a sinister smile, and remarks, "Here's some gang justice for you!" As the gangster with the pistol chambers a round - ZIP! A black metal star strikes deep into the thug's hand and he drops the gun. Bossman and his crew spin around to see Carl, Morgan, Barry and Eli attack. The Ninjans attack from four sides - the Ninjans deliver strikes, blows and kicks that decimate the thug ranks, and the gangsters fall like dominoes! Only four NWG are left - Bossman and three of his henchmen. Barry, Morgan and Eli, keep their swords on the three underlings. Carl strides up to confront Bossman face to face - and stares at him, "Now, we can fight! No army of thugs - just you and me - man to man!" Bossman smirks, cracks his neck, takes a Martial Arts stance and replies with bravado, "Bring it on old man! You've never fought someone like me before!" Carl signals and the Ninjans take the thugs off to the side to leave room for Carl and Bossman to fight. Bossman scowls and rips off his top to reveal his muscular body with chiseled abs. The gang leader motions with his hands at Carl to come on! Carl circles to the right - then circles to the left - he releases a roundhouse which Bossman aptly deflects. Bossman laughs and taunts, "Not bad old man - but not quick enough!" Carl swiftly lunges in with a Tiger punch that hits Bossman directly in the face. POW! Bossman wipes his lip and spits out blood and smirks. Suddenly, Bossman flips and kicks Carl in the chest to knock him down into the dirt. Carl quickly gets to his feet. Bossman rushes in with a flurry of punches and strikes that Carl blocks and deflects, but one of Bossman's punches get through and strikes Carl and disorients him. Carl stumbles, temporarily stunned!   Bossman sees his opportunity and quickly attacks with a powerful kick that sends Carl flying backwards into the dirt. Carl starts to get up and Bossman rushes in with a mighty kick to Carl's stomach. Bossman repeatedly kicks the downed Ninjan again and again. Barry stirs to help Carl but Morgan motions for him to hold off. On the ground, Carl lifts his eye to scan about, and Bossman kicks Carl in the side of the face. Bossman steps back and gloats to see Carl sprawled out on the ground - bloody, bruised, beaten and weak. Bossman mocks, "Lost your skills old man? (Eyes Carl) You're not so tough! ... I'll kill you like I killed your old lady!" Carl is SHOCKED! He lays motionless for a couple seconds, the pain of the news strikes him to the core of his being. Morgan, Barry and Eli are horrified to hear of Kathy's death! Barry raises his sword to attack Bossman, Carl sees it and motions for Barry to stop - No! Carl stares at Bossman with righteous anger and rage. He lifts himself up and faces the arrogant thug. Carl points his finger and declares, "Today

- there will be justice for my wife - and justice for our Indian lands that you have defiled!" Bossman is livid and runs at Carl with series of swings and punches. Carl ducks and repeatedly strikes Bossman in the upper torso leaving the huge thug in severe excruciating pain! Bossman keeps flailing and punching away. Carl steps in and delvers a series of powerful blows to Bossman's groin, chest and back. Bossman steps back and briefly teeters, greatly weakened. He's dizzy and shakes his head. Blood seeps from the corner of his lip. Bossman wipes his mouth and looks at the blood on his hand. He coughs, grabs his chest and struggles to move but can't. The bewildered thug looks at Carl and yells, "What did you do old man? - What did you do to me?" Carl slowly walks up just out of arm's reach and replies, "Your body is going to lock up - and there's nothing you can do about it! You won't escape the Police anymore!" Bossman gasps as he stares at Carl, the big thug clutches his legs and chest as he strains and struggles. Carl, his fellow Ninjans, and the three remaining thugs, watch in silence as Bossman contorts and desperately fights to move but can't. Bossman's vision becomes blurred and he wipes his eyes, his power wanes and he wobbles on his feet - he loses strength and crumbles to his knees in the dirt. Bossman groans as he stares ahead and falls face-first into the dirt - locked stiff as a statue! Carl steps up to the fallen gangster, reaches into his tunic and brings out a small black feather and lets it fall onto the gangster's body. Carl looks over at the Ninjans. Morgan points and asks, "What about these three?" Carl replies, "Tie them up (eyes thugs) Can't tell who will find the first - the Cops or the coyotes!" The three thugs become scared and plead as the Ninjans bind their hands and feet. Once secured, The Ninjans put the three young men up high on a big metal drum well off the ground. Carl looks at the gangster trio and remarks, "The coyotes won't get you up here! We may live in the wilderness - but we're not savages!" Carl and the fellow Ninjans walk to their hidden vehicles. Barry and Eli help Steve to their truck. At their vehicles, the Ninjans exchange glances, and Carl remarks, "Thank you! I'm in your debt!" The others exchange looks and Morgan replies, "We're brothers! - Black Feathers!" Carl smiles and nods, and the five Ninjans get into their cars and drive away from the abandoned factory. As the Ninjans drive off into the desert, they can see the gangster's vehicles burning in the background, the flames light up the dusk.

Some time later, Police cars, SWAT and Paramedics arrive on scene. The Officers comb the area and find the factory grounds and buildings littered with injured and unconscious gangsters. Most of the thugs are beaten and wounded and need assistance from the Police and medical personnel. Officers rescue the three bound gangsters atop the high steel drum. As the Police help get them down, the trio speak about their ordeal and gesture wildly about samurai warriors. The Police Officers cuff the trio ignoring their story as wild imagination or a drug induced high. The gangsters are all handcuffed and rounded up in a group and guarded by armed Officers. Paramedics tend to those needing medical attention. A team of Officers find Bossman's locked body amid the grounds of the scrap yard. The brute is alive and totally immobilized. A Policeman bends down to examine the small black feather and picks it up. He remarks to his partner, "Huh! A little black feather. What do you make of this?" The other Officer looks at the feather and replies, "Likely a bird flew by - maybe a Starling." Four Officers lift and carry Bossman over to where all the other gangsters are corralled. The four Policemen lay Bossman's stiff rigid body on the ground - Bossman is alert and aware but he can't move or say a thing! Chief Rogers, the other Commanders walk around to inspect the crime scene. The leaders watch as Officers collect evidence, mark bullet casings, and inspect burnt out vehicles. As Chief Rogers and the other Commanders tour the crime site, a senior Officer with a clipboard approaches and shows them the collected data. Police Chief Rogers scans the details and remarks, "Whoever or whatever did this - gave us all the criminals! We have the entire Northwest Gang and its leader in custody!" Chief Rogers and the other Commanders smile broadly, then Chief Rogers and the Commanders continue their survey of the grounds. The old Steel Mill and property shimmer in an eerie glow as gang vehicles burn, and the flashing lights from Police cruisers and ambulances illuminate the night sky.

CHAPTER THIRTY
A Sweet Tearful Good Bye

Carl and a Morgue Attendant walk to a stainless steel examination table, where a body lays underneath a white linen sheet. Carl's eyes sweep up and down the shrouded human form of a female. The Attendant pulls the sheet cover down to reveal the face and shoulders of the deceased. The man respectfully asks, "Is this your wife?" Carl swallows hard and fights back breaking down crying, and softly replies, "Yes! That's my wife Kathy!" The Morgue Attendant looks at Carl with sympathy, "I'm sorry Mr. Long Grass! (Pause) She died on route to the hospital. The Paramedics tried but couldn't revive her! - I'm sorry!" The Attendant covers Kathy's lifeless body - and Carl turns away and tears stream down his face, he sobs! Carl takes a deep breath and walks toward the Morgue entrance door, grabs the handle - then turns to look at the covered body of his deceased wife, Kathy. Carl stands motionless for a minute, then he clicks the door handle and exits the room.

At the funeral Service, Kathy's body lays serene in a polished rosewood open casket. Bouquets and wreaths of flowers from family and friends flank each side of the casket to honour and pay tribute to her memory. The Funeral Home's viewing room is filled with tearful people giving hugs of support, respectful handshakes, and gentle pats of condolence. Carl and Tommy are dressed in white shirt and black suit, and stand beside the casket. A large framed photograph of Kathy with her cascading hair and beautiful smile sits in a picture stand a few feet from the coffin. The people that line up to pay their respects file past Kathy's lovely photo - many are brought to tears. She was well known and dearly loved as a fine lady that lived on the Indian Reserve. Her legacy of helping children read at the Library, volunteering with the local Food Bank, and visiting residents at the

Nursing Home, won her great respect and admiration throughout the community. Now, it was time for the community people to say their good bye to her. Kathy's siblings dressed in black and with swollen eyes from crying, sit in the front row of chairs in the viewing room, lending their presence and support to Carl and Tommy. As the individuals, couples and families file by the open casket to set their eyes upon Kathy one last time, Carl shakes their hand for showing their support, Tommy stands quiet and still on the other side of his grandfather. Carl glances at the front portion of the seating and sees his friends Morgan, Steve, Barry and Eli with their families. Carl nods to his old friends and they nod in quiet respect. Tommy glances around and spots Officer Stibbs dressed in a dark blue suit and tie, and the Officer gives a polite gentle wave to his young friend. The Officer takes a chair among those already seated. The Funeral Attendant quietly approaches and gently touches Carl's arm to indicate it is time to be seated. As Carl and Tommy sit with family in the front row, The Funeral Attendant respectfully closes the lid of the casket, and sets a beautiful bouquet of flowers on top the coffin. All eyes turn toward the Minister as he steps behind the podium that's set to one side of the closed casket and flowers. The Minister opens his Bible and looks out at the family and assembled friends and speaks, "Dear beloved, we are gathered here this day to honour and say our final good bye to Kathy Long Grass, - a loving wife, a caring grandmother, a dear sister, gracious aunt, helpful neighbour, and well-respected lady in the community. As the Funeral Home organist begins to play, the Minister encourages everyone in the room, "As the grieving family remain seated, let everyone rise and together we will sing the timeless hymn: Amazing Grace." Everyone stands, except Carl, Tommy and relatives; and the people raise their voices as the organist plays the well known melody.

Following the Funeral Home Service, at the Cemetery there is a long line of vehicles parked on the Cemetery's paved lane near the tombstones. The back door of the Hearst is open and the Minister and Funeral Attendants stand to one side as eight Pall Bearers lift and support the coffin. The Minister leads the Procession as the Pall Bearers carry the casket to the open gravesite; while Carl, Tommy and Kathy's relatives follow. The rest of the Funeral attendees walk behind the relatives. The burial Procession reaches the open grave and stop - the Pall Bearers position and carefully lower the casket onto the strapping that suspends the coffin above the open grave. Carl, Tommy and

Kathy's siblings sit down on a row of wooden folding chairs placed for the graveside ceremony. Morgan , Barry, Steve and Eli and their families stand close by. The friends and supporters gather around to fill in spots here and there. Tommy stares off into space. Morgan places his hand on Tommy's shoulder for assurance. Carl and Tommy look at each other - then turn their eyes toward Kathy's coffin before them. The framed photo of Kathy with her radiant smile sits atop the middle of the casket. The Minister opens his thin leather Bible and speaks in a comforting tone, "We enter this world with nothing and we leave this life the same - taking nothing with us. Kathy as a Christian, has gone to Heaven to live in Eternal Peace and Joy with her Heavenly Father. This is the Hope of all believers in Jesus!" The Minister steps beside the closed casket and brings out a small slender glass tube from his jacket, opens the top and pours white sand in the form of a Cross on top the coffin, and remarks, "Ashes to ashes, dust to dust, we commit our sister Kathy to the Lord, her spirit rests with God in Heaven, and her physical body will be raised to eternal life in the Resurrection!" The Minister steps away from the Casket and looks at the Funeral Attendants and nods. A Funeral Attendant retrieves Kathy's framed photo and brings it to Carl. The man steps back and looks out at the gathered friends and supporters and remarks, "We will be lowering the casket now. The Graveside Service concludes at this time and we wish to thank you for your attendance and support. As we escort the family to the Funeral cars, we kindly ask that you make your way back to your vehicles, and please join us for refreshments back at the Funeral Home Meeting Room. Thank You!" The Funeral Attendant gently motions with his hand and Carl and Tommy and Kathy's relatives stand and follow the Attendants to the waiting Funeral cars. The rest of the people disperse and make their way to their parked vehicles. Walking toward the Funeral Home's black limousine, Carl and Tommy exchange eye contact, the grandfather sees his grandson is very quiet and tight-lipped. Carl speaks softly, "I know you really loved your grandma - and you'll miss her very much!" Tommy looks at his grandpa with tears welling up in his eyes, "It's not fair! Grandma was a kind sweet lady. Why did she have to die?" Carl puts his arm around Tommy and draws him close and replies, "Evil people do evil things! It's our job as good people to stand against them - that's what your grandma did!" The Funeral Attendant opens the rear passenger door of the limousine and Carl and Tommy get seated inside - then the Attendant closes the car door.

Three months have passed since the funeral. Carl, Tommy and Sarah, stand before Kathy's grave, and Carl sets a container with a lovely bouquet of flowers in front Kathy's tombstone. Carl is silent and still as he stands at Kathy's grave. Tommy steps beside his grandpa with a serene smile and comments, "Grandma always loved those kind of flowers. She'd be happy!" Carl looks over at his grandson, smiles and pulls Tommy close. Sarah watches the tender scene with watery eyes.

CHAPTER THIRTY-ONE

One Year Later

Tommy races in through the front door with his backpack and a large manila envelope. He puts his knapsack in an armchair and opens the large envelop and takes out the official paper with the High School logo - it reads REPORT CARD A+ …… Tommy smiles wide and sets the academic report in the middle of the table. He turns and grabs his backpack, goes into his room and tosses the backpack in a corner. With excitement in his eyes, he walks to a tall black cabinet and opens it.

Carl stands in the big backyard dressed in his black Ninjan outfit and holds two sheathed Katana swords. He hears the house back door open and turns to see Tommy standing in the back entrance dressed in a white Ninjan outfit. Tommy springs off the back steps and bounds toward his grandfather and stops a few feet away. Tommy bows and Carl bows in return. Carl smiles at Tommy's enthusiasm and tosses him one of the sheathed Kanata swords. Tommy catches the weapon and admires the white pearl inlay of the scabbard. With one hand holding the scabbard - Tommy uses his other hand to draw out the highly polished steel blade - slow and respectful. Tommy fully extends the sword blade and it gleams in the afternoon sun. Carl looks at his grandson and remarks, "Today, Tommy - you start your Ninjan training!" Tommy lowers the blade by his side and bows and replies, "Yes Sensi!" Carl gazes tenderly at Tommy, smiles and remarks, "Let's begin!" Tommy positions himself a few feet adjacent to his grandfather. The teenager keenly watches Carl's every step and move of the sword. The old Ninjan Master and the young apprentice flow in unison - the two swing and move their swords in a beautiful ballet of blades! As the afternoon sun casts sunlight on everything, Carl and Tommy are bathed in a golden glow.

Across the Indian Reservation, kids are returning from school, parents arrive home from their workday, moms and dads are preparing meals, and people get supplies at local stores. Morgan sits in his Dojo Office doing administration and clerical duties for a pile of new applications. Barry works in his busy auto shop to tighten a bolt on an engine. Steve just completes a welding job and lifts up his welder's mask to inspect the metal parts. On the outskirts of town, Eli stands in the corral as he breaks in a wild young colt. The Indian Reserve and surrounding desert region is full of life, of both human and creature. A rabbit runs through the sage brush, a ground hog raise its head from its burrow, and up on higher elevation, a black eagle with wings extended, swoops in to land on the branch of a tall pine tree and cries out - its call echoes across the rugged wilderness.

As Carl and Tommy train - Carl moves his sword with grace and power - swift and precise! Tommy does his best to keep up with the Ninjan Master. The two warriors move in tandem - grandfather and grandson smiling! Beyond the backyard, the tall grass sways and bends in the wind. As Carl and Tommy train with swords, at the house in the background, Carl's bedroom window is open, and a large black feather on a leather cord spins and twirls in the breeze.

THE END

ACKNOWLEDGEMENTS

The author wishes to acknowledge
and give credit to

Google.com
Wikipedia.org
History.com
Encyclopedia.com
Thoughtco.com

for the online sources
used for research in writing

Chapter Five:

A New Century And A Whirl Through Time